MORE PRAISE FOR
I Wish Someone Were Waiting for Me Somewhere

"Some books are so successful they give you the illusion that the author is your friend. Anna Gavalda is a distant descendant of Dorothy Parker."
— *Voici*

"Anna Gavalda swings her very short stories from slightly acidic charms to the cutting verve." — *24Heures*

"Without flourishes, in a lively style, often funny, at times serious, Anna Gavalda discusses small pieces of life. Twelve snapshots that speak of coming-apart love, of met-again love, of aborted love, of unknown love." — *Biba*

"We immediately enter [Gavalda's] lively universe, which can also turn out to be a whirling, dark, and sharp world."
— *Vital*

"A collection that derives a wicked pleasure from domesticating the most diverse characters in contemporary society."
— *Les Inrockuptibles*

"It's the sheer variety that hits you in Anna Gavalda's wonderful collection of short stories. Parisian chic or drab provincialism, poignant or hilarious, sophistication or farce, Gavalda writes with tantalizing ease both from male and female perspectives, whatever their age and occupation. A highly enjoyable read, these lively and visual stories linger in the mind."
— *French Book News*

I Wish Someone Were Waiting for Me Somewhere

ANNA GAVALDA

Translated from the French by
Karen L. Marker

RIVERHEAD BOOKS
NEW YORK

Riverhead Books
Published by The Berkley Publishing Group
A division of Penguin Group (USA) Inc.
375 Hudson Street
New York, New York 10014

First published in France by Le Dilettante as *Je voudrais que
quelqu'un m'attende quelque part*, 1999
Copyright © Le Dilettante, 1999
Translation copyright © Penguin Group (USA) Inc., 2003
Book design by Tiffany Estreicher

First Riverhead trade paperback edition: December 2003

Library of Congress Cataloging-in-Publication Data
Gavalda, Anna, 1970–
[Je voudrais que quelqu'un m'attende quelque part. English]
I wish someone were waiting for me somewhere / Anna Gavalda ; translated from
the French by Karen L. Marker.
p.   cm.
ISBN 1-57322-355-7
I. Marker, Karen L.   II. Title.
PQ2667.A97472J4 2003
843'.92–dc22   2003058690

Printed in the United States of America

10   9   8   7   6   5   4   3   2   1

I wish someone were waiting for me somewhere.

For my sister Marianne.

CONTENTS

Courting Rituals of the
Saint-Germain-des-Prés
1

Pregnant
15

This Man and This Woman
31

The Opel Touch
35

Amber
47

Leave
59

Lead Story
79

Catgut
93

Junior
101

For Years
118

Clic-Clac
138

Epilogue
171

I Wish Someone Were Waiting for Me Somewhere

Courting Rituals of the
Saint-Germain-des-Prés

Saint-Germain-des-Prés? . . . I know what you're going to say: "God, that whole Left Bank thing is so clichéd. Françoise Sagan did it long before you, *chérie*—and sooo much better! Haven't you read *Bonjour Tristesse*!?"

I know.

But what do you expect? . . . I'm not sure any of this would've happened to me on Boulevard de Clichy or in some other part of Paris. That's just the way it is. *C'est la vie.*

So keep your thoughts to yourself and hear me out, because something tells me this story's going to amuse you.

You love this kind of sentimental fluff—having someone make your heart beat faster with these evenings full of promise, these men who want you to think they're single and a little down on their luck.

I know you love it. It's perfectly normal. Still, you can't

read Harlequin romances while you're sitting at Café Lipp or Deux Magots. No, of course you can't.

So, this morning, I passed a man on Boulevard Saint-Germain.

I was going up the street and he was coming down it. We were on the even-numbered side, which is more elegant.

I saw him coming from a distance. I don't know just what it was, maybe the carefree way he walked, or the way the skirt of his coat swung out in front of him . . . anyhow, I was twenty meters away and I already knew I couldn't go wrong.

Sure enough, when he passes, I see him look at me. I shoot him a mischievous smile—kind of like one of Cupid's arrows, only more discreet.

He smiles back.

I keep walking, still smiling, and think of Baudelaire's *To a Passerby*. (What with that reference to Sagan earlier, by now you must have realized I'm what they call the literary type!) I slow down, trying to remember the lines of the poem . . . *Tall, slender, in deep mourning* . . . after that I don't know what . . . then . . . *A woman passed, with a sumptuous hand, raising, dangling the embroidered hem* . . . and at the end . . . *O you whom I had loved, O you who knew it.*

That gets me every time.

And during all this, pure and simple, I can sense the

gaze of my Saint Sebastian (a reference to the arrow, see? stay with me, okay?!) still on my back. It warms my shoulder blades deliciously, but I'd rather die than turn around. That would ruin the poem.

I'd stopped at the curb up by rue des Saints-Pères, watching the stream of cars for a chance to cross.

For the record: No self-respecting *Parisienne* on Boulevard Saint-Germain would ever cross on the white lines when the light is red. A self-respecting *Parisienne* watches the stream of cars and steps out, fully aware of the risk she's taking.

To die for the window display at Paule Ka. Delicious.

I'm finally stepping out when a voice holds me back. I'm not going to say, "a hot, virile voice" just to make you happy, because that's not how it was. Just a voice.

"Excuse me . . ."

I turn around. And who's there? . . . Why, my scrumptious prey from a minute ago.

I might as well tell you right now, from that moment on: screw Baudelaire.

"I was wondering if you'd like to have dinner with me tonight. . . ."

In my head, I think, "How romantic . . ." But I answer:

"That's a little fast, don't you think?"

Without missing a beat, he says (and I swear this is the truth):

"Well, yes, I'll grant you that. But when I saw you walking away, I said to myself, 'This is ridiculous. Here's this woman I pass in the street. I smile at her, she smiles at me, we brush past one another, and we're about to lose each other. . . . It's ridiculous—no, really, it's absurd.'"

". . ."

"What do you think? Does that seem like total nonsense to you, what I just said?"

"No, no, not at all."

I was beginning to feel a little uneasy. . . .

"Well, then? . . . What do you say? Let's say we meet here, tonight, at nine o'clock? Right at this spot."

Get ahold of yourself, girl. If you're going to have dinner with every man you smile at, you'll never get out of the gate. . . .

"Give me one good reason to say yes."

"One good reason . . . God . . . that's hard. . . ."

I watch him, amused.

And then, without warning, he takes my hand. "I think I've found a more or less suitable reason. . . ."

He passes my hand over his scruffy cheek.

"One good reason. There: Say yes so I'll have a reason to shave. . . . You know, I think I look a lot better when I've shaved."

And he gives me back my arm.

"Yes," I say.

"Good, then we're on! Can I walk you across the street? I don't want to lose you now."

This time I'm the one watching him walk off. He must be stroking his cheeks like a guy who's struck a good deal. . . .

I'm sure he's enormously pleased with himself. He should be.

Late afternoon and a little nervous, I have to admit.

Beat at my own game. Should've read the rule book.

A little nervous, like a debutante having a bad-hair day.

A little nervous, like someone on the threshold of a love story.

At work, I answer the phone, I send faxes, I finish a mock-up for the photo researcher (what did you expect . . . a pretty, vivacious girl who sends faxes from Saint-Germain-des-Prés inevitably works in publishing . . .).

The tips of my fingers are ice-cold and everyone has to tell me everything twice.

Breathe, girl, breathe. . . .

At dusk, the street is quieter and the cars all have their headlights on.

The café tables are being brought in from the sidewalks. There are people on the church square waiting to meet up with friends, and at the Beauregard people are lining up to see the latest Woody Allen film.

I don't want to be the first one there. It wouldn't be right. In fact, I decide to go a little late. Better to make him want me a little.

So I go have a little pick-me-up to get the blood flowing back to my fingers.

Not at the Deux Magots, it's a little uncouth in the evenings—no one but fat American women on the lookout for the ghost of Simone de Beauvoir. I take rue Saint-Benoît. The Chiquito will do just fine.

I push the door open, and right away there's the smell of beer and stale tobacco . . . the ding ding of the pinball machine . . . the hieratic bar owner with her dyed hair and nylon blouse, support bra showing . . . the sound of the Vincennes night race playing in the background . . . some masons in stained overalls, putting off the hour of solitude or the old ball and chain . . . and the old regulars, fingers yellow, annoying everyone with their rents that haven't changed since '48. Bliss.

The men at the bar turn around from time to time and giggle among themselves like a bunch of schoolboys. My legs are in the aisle. They're very long. The aisle is kind of narrow and my skirt is very short. I see their stooped backs jiggling in fits and jerks.

I smoke a cigarette, sending the smoke out far in front of me. I stare off into space. Beautiful Day has won it in the final straightaway, ten-to-one odds, I learn.

I remember I've got *Kennedy and Me* in my bag, and I wonder if I wouldn't be better off staying here.

Salt pork with lentils and a half pitcher of rosé . . . wouldn't that be nice. . . .

But I pull myself together. You're there, over my shoulder, hoping for love (or less? or more? or not exactly?) with me, and I'm not going to leave you stranded with the owner of the Chiquito. That would be a little harsh.

I go out, cheeks rosy, and the cold whips my legs.

He's there, at the corner of rue des Saint-Pères, waiting for me. He sees me and walks over.

"I was worried—I was afraid you wouldn't come. I saw my reflection in a window, and I couldn't help but admire my cheeks, all nice and smooth. So I was worried."

"I'm sorry. I was waiting for the end of the Vincennes race and I lost track of time."

"Who won?

"You bet?"

"No."

"Beautiful Day."

"Of course. I should've known." He smiles, taking my arm.

We walk in silence as far as rue Saint-Jacques. From time to time, he steals a look at me, examining my profile, but I know what he's really wondering just then is whether I'm wearing pantyhose or thigh highs.

Patience, my good man, patience. . . .

"I'm going to take you to a place I really like."

I can picture it now . . . the kind of place where the waiters are relaxed but obsequious, smiling at him with a knowing air: "Good eeevening, monsieur . . . (*there she is then, the latest . . . you know, I liked the brunette from last time better . . .*) . . . the little table in the back as usual, monsieur?" . . . bowing as he shows the way (*. . . but where does he dig up all these babes? . . .*), ". . . May I take your coats? Veeery well."

He digs them up in the street, stupid.

But it's nothing like that.

He holds the door, letting me lead the way into a little

wine bistro, and a bored-looking waiter asks us if we smoke. That's all.

He hung our things on a coatrack. In the half second he paused when he caught sight of the softness of my bust, I knew he didn't regret the little nick he'd given himself under the chin earlier, when his hands betrayed him while he was shaving.

We drank extraordinary wine out of fat wineglasses. We ate relatively subtle things, conceived precisely so as not to spoil the aroma of our nectars.

A bottle of Côte de Nuits, Gevrey-Chambertin 1986. Baby Jesus in velvet britches.

The man sitting across from me crinkles his eyes as he drinks.

I'm getting to know him better now.

He's wearing a gray cashmere turtleneck sweater. An old one. It's got elbow patches and a small tear near the right wrist. His twentieth birthday present, maybe . . . I can just see his mother, troubled by his disappointed pout, telling him, "You won't be sorry, go ahead, try it on . . ." as she kisses him and strokes his back.

His jacket is unpretentious—it looks like any old tweed—but, as it's me and my lynx eyes, I can tell it's tailor-made. At Old England, the labels are bigger when the merchandise goes out straight from the Capucines workshops, and I saw the label when he leaned down to pick up his napkin.

His napkin that he'd dropped on purpose in order to settle once and for all this question of the pantyhose, I imagine.

He talks to me about a lot of things but never about himself. He always has a little trouble holding on to his train of thought when I let my fingers trail across my neck. He says, "And you?" and I don't ever talk about myself, either.

As we wait for dessert, my foot touches his ankle.

He puts his hand on mine and pulls it back suddenly because the sorbets have arrived.

He says something, but his words don't make a sound and I don't hear anything.

We're all worked up.

Horrors. His cell phone just rang.

As though they were one, all eyes in the restaurant fix on him as he deftly switches it off. He's certainly just wasted a lot of very good wine. Half-gulped mouthfuls caught in rasping throats. People choking, their fingers clenching knife handles or the creases of starched napkins.

Those damn things. There always has to be one, no matter where, no matter when.

The boor.

He's embarrassed. He's suddenly a little warm in his mommy's cashmere.

He nods his head at this group and that, as though to express his dismay. He looks at me and his shoulders have slumped a little.

"I'm sorry. . . ." He smiles at me again, but it's less self-assured, you could say.

I tell him, "It's no big deal. It's not like we're at the movies. Someday I'm going to kill someone. Some man or woman who answers the phone in the middle of the show. When you read it in the news briefs, you'll know it was me. . . ."

"I will."

"You read the news briefs?"

"No. But I'm going to start, now that I have a chance of finding you there."

The sorbets were, how should I put it . . . delicious.

Reinvigorated, my prince charming came to sit next to me when the coffee was served.

So close that now he's sure: I'm wearing thigh highs. He felt the little hook at the top of my thigh.

I know that at that moment, he doesn't know where he lives anymore.

He lifts my hair and kisses my neck, in the little hollow spot at the back.

He whispers into my ear that he loves Boulevard Saint-Germain, he loves burgundy and black currant sorbets.

I kiss his little cut. After all the time I've waited for this moment, I really get into it.

The coffee, the bill, the tip, our coats, all that is just details, details, details. Details that get in our way.

Our hearts are slamming against our chests.

He hands me my black coat and then . . .

I admire the work of the artist, hats off, it's very discreet, barely noticeable, it's very well calculated and perfectly executed: in placing the coat on my bare shoulders, proffered to him and soft as silk, he finds the half second necessary and the perfect tilt toward the inside pocket of his jacket to glance at the message screen on his cell phone.

I come to my senses. All at once.

Traitor.

Ingrate.

What in heaven's name were you thinking?!

What could possibly have distracted you when my shoulders were so round and warm and your hand was so close!?

What business was more important than my breasts offered to your view?

How could you let yourself be sidetracked while I was waiting for your breath on my back?

Couldn't you have waited to mess with the damn thing later, after you'd made love to me?

I button my coat all the way up.

In the street, I'm cold, I'm tired, and I feel sick.

I ask him to walk me to the nearest taxi stand.

He's in a panic.

Call 911, bud, you've got what you need.

But no. He's a stoic.

As if nothing has happened. As in, I'm walking a good friend to her taxi, I'm rubbing her sleeves to warm her, and I'm chatting about the Paris night.

Classy almost to the end, I have to grant him that.

Before I climb into a black Mercedes taxi with Val-de-Marne plates, he says:

"But . . . we'll see each other again, won't we? I don't

even know where you live. . . . Give me something, an
address, a phone number. . . ."

He tears a scrap of paper out of his agenda and scribbles
some numbers.

"Take this. The first number, that's home, the second,
that's my cell, you can reach me there anytime. . . ."

That much I'd figured out.

"Don't hesitate, no matter when, okay? . . . I'll be waiting
to hear from you."

I ask the driver to let me out at the top of the boulevard.
I need to walk.

I kick some imaginary tin cans.

I hate cell phones, I hate Sagan, I hate Baudelaire and
all those charlatans.

I hate my pride.

Pregnant

They're nuts, these women who want a baby. Nuts.

They barely even find out they're pregnant before they open wide the floodgates: of love, of love, of love.

They never close them again afterward.

They're nuts.

She's like the rest of them. She thinks she's pregnant. She supposes. She imagines. She isn't sure-sure yet but almost.

She waits a few more days. To see.

She knows that a Predictor pharmacy test costs nine euros. She remembers from the first baby.

She says to herself: I'll wait two more days and I'll do the test.

Of course she doesn't wait. She says to herself: What's

nine euros when maybe, just maybe, I'm pregnant? What's nine euros when in two minutes I could know?

Nine euros to finally throw open the floodgates because it's beginning to cave at the back, it's boiling, it's swirling and it's making her a little sick to her stomach.

She runs to the pharmacy. Not her usual pharmacy, one more discreet where no one knows her. She assumes a detached air, a pregnancy test please, but her heart's already thumping.

She goes back to the house. She waits. She prolongs the exquisite agony. The test is there, in her bag on the table in the entryway, and as for her, she's a bit restless. She remains master of the situation. She folds laundry. She goes to day care to pick up her child. She chats with the other moms. She laughs. She's in a good mood.

She fixes the after-school snack. She butters slices of bread. She really gets into it. She licks the spoon from the jam. She can't stop kissing her child. Everywhere. On the neck. On the cheeks. On the head.

He says stop, Mom, you're driving me nuts.

She gets him settled in front of a box of LEGOs and she lingers a little while, getting in his way.

She goes downstairs. She tries to ignore her bag but she can't. She stops. She picks up the test.

She loses patience with the packaging. She tears off the wrapper with her teeth. She'll read the instructions in a minute. She pees on the top of the doohickey. She puts it back in its case, the way you cap a ballpoint pen. She holds it in her hand and it's all warm.

She sets it down somewhere.

She reads the instructions. You must wait four minutes and check the test windows. If both windows are pink, madame, your urine is full of hCG (human chorionic gonadotropin); if the two windows are pink, madame, you are pregnant.

Four minutes is such a long time. She drinks a cup of tea while waiting.

She sets the kitchen timer for a soft-boiled egg. Four minutes . . . there.

She doesn't fiddle with the test. She burns her lips on her tea.

She looks at the cracks in the kitchen and she wonders what on earth she's going to manage to fix for dinner.

She doesn't wait the four minutes, anyway there's no reason to. You can already read the result. She's pregnant.

She knew it.

She flings the test to the very bottom of the trash can. She arranges other empty packages on top to cover it completely. For the moment, it's her secret.

She feels better.

She breathes in deeply, she takes in air. She knew it.

It was just to be sure. That's that, the floodgates are open. Now she can think about other things.

She'll never think about anything else again.

Look at any pregnant woman: You think that she's crossing the street or that she's working or even that she's talking to you. Wrong. She's thinking about her baby.

She'll never admit it but not one minute goes by in those nine months that she's not thinking about her baby.

Okay so she listens to you, but she doesn't really hear you. She nods her head but in truth, she couldn't care less.

She imagines it. Five millimeters: a grain of wheat. A centimeter: a pasta shell. Five centimeters: this eraser sitting on the desk. Twenty centimeters and four and a half months: her hand wide open.

There's nothing there. You can't see anything and yet she touches her belly often.

But no, it's not her belly that she touches, it's him. Exactly like when she runs her fingers through the hair of the older one. Just the same.

She told her husband. She'd dreamed up a whole host of imaginative ways to announce the news.

Various settings, tones of voice, repeat-the-sounding-joy . . . or then again not.

She told him one evening, in the dark, when their legs

were intertwined but just for sleeping. She told him: I'm pregnant, and he kissed her ear. So much the better, he answered.

She told her other child too. You know there's a baby in Mommy's belly. A little brother or a little sister like Pierre's mommy. And you'll be able to push the baby's stroller, like Pierre.

He lifted her sweater and he said: Where is he? He's not there, the baby?

She scoured her bookshelves to find *Nine Months to Motherhood* by Laurence Pernoud. The book's a little worn—it served her sister-in-law and a girlfriend in the meantime.

Right away, she goes to the photos in the middle to look at them all over again.

The chapter is called "Images of life before birth," from "The ovum surrounded by spermatozoids" to "Six months: he sucks his thumb."

She scrutinizes the itty-bitty hands, so transparent that you can see the blood vessels, and then the eyebrows—in some shots, you can already see the eyebrows.

Next she goes straight to the chapter "When will I give birth?" There's a table that gives the estimated date of birth. ("Numbers in black: date of the first day of menstruation. Numbers in color: probable date of delivery.")

That gives us a baby November 29. What's November 29? She raises her eyes and grabs hold of the post office calendar hanging next to the microwave . . . November 29 . . . Saint Saturninus.

Saturninus, now there's a name for you! she says to herself, smiling.

She sets the book down haphazardly. It's not likely she'll open it again. Because for the rest (how should you eat? backaches, pregnancy-related breakouts, stretch marks, sexual relations, will your child be normal? how should you prepare for delivery? the truth about the pain, etc.), all that, she scoffs at a little, or rather, it doesn't interest her. She's confident.

In the afternoons she's asleep on her feet, and she eats huge Russian pickles at every meal.

Before the end of the third month comes the first mandatory visit to the gynecologist. For the blood tests, the social security papers, the declaration of pregnancy to send to her employer.

She goes during her lunch hour. She's more emotional than she seems.

She sees the same doctor who brought her first child into the world.

They talk a little about this and that: and your husband, the job? and your work, it's coming along? and your children, school? and that other school, do you think?

Next to the examining table is the ultrasound. She settles in. The screen is still dark but she can't stop looking at it.

First and foremost, he has her listen to the beating of the invisible heart.

The sound is set fairly loud, and it resonates throughout the whole room:

boom-boom-boom-boom-boom-boom

What an idiot, she already has tears in her eyes.

And then he shows her the baby.

A tiny little fellow who moves his arms and his legs. Ten centimeters and forty-five grams. His spinal column is clearly visible, you could even count the vertebrae.

Her mouth must be wide open, but she doesn't say a thing.

The doctor makes jokes. He says: ha, I was sure of it, that shuts up even the biggest chatterboxes.

While she gets dressed, he puts together a little file with photos that came out of the machine. And a little later, when she's in her car, before she starts the engine, she'll spend a long time looking at these photos and while she's learning them by heart, you won't hear the sound of her breathing.

Weeks have passed and her belly's gotten bigger. Her breasts, too. Now, she wears a 36C. Unthinkable.

She went to a maternity shop to buy clothes that fit. She splurged. She chose a very pretty and rather expensive dress for her cousin's wedding in late August. A linen dress with little mother-of-pearl buttons all the way down. She hesitated for a long time because she's not sure she'll ever have another child. And then, obviously, it's a bit pricey. . . .

She mulls it over in the fitting room, she gets bogged down in calculations. When she comes back out, with the dress in her arms and hesitation on her face, the saleswoman says: go ahead, treat yourself! Okay, so you won't be able to wear it for long, but what a pleasure! . . . Besides, a pregnant woman should always have her way. She says it in a joking tone but all the same, she's a good saleswoman.

She thinks of that once she's in the street with the big impractical bag in her hand. She really has to pee. As usual.

Plus, it's an important wedding for her because her son is the ring bearer. It's stupid but it makes her really happy.

Another topic of infinite deliberations is the sex of the baby.

Should they, yes or no, ask whether it's a girl or a boy?

The fifth month is coming up and with it the second ultrasound, the one that tells all.

At work, she has a lot of worrisome problems to solve and decisions to make every other minute.

She makes them. That's what she's paid for.

But this . . . she doesn't know.

For the first one, she'd wanted to know, it's true. But this time, she really couldn't care less if it's a girl or a boy. Really.

All right, she won't ask.

"You're sure?" said the doctor. She doesn't know anymore. "Listen, I won't say anything and we'll see if you can see anything for yourself."

He moves the transducer slowly over her gel-covered belly. Sometimes he stops, he takes measurements, he comments, sometimes he moves it quickly, smiling. Finally he says: okay, you can get back up.

"Well?" he asks.

She says that she has an inkling but she isn't sure. "And what's your inkling?" Well . . . she thought she saw evidence of a little boy, didn't she? . . .

"Ah, I don't know," he answers, making a teasing face.

She wants to grab him by the shirt and shake him so that he'll tell, but no. It's a surprise.

In the summertime, a huge belly, it keeps you warm. Not to mention the nights. You sleep so badly, no position is comfortable. But fine.

The date of the wedding is approaching. Tension mounts in the family. She offers to take care of the bouquets. It's the perfect job for a cetacean like her. They'll put her right in the middle of things, the boys will bring her whatever she needs and she'll make it all as beautiful as can be.

While she waits she runs to shoe stores looking for close-toed white sandals. The bride wants to see them all wearing the same shoes. How practical. Impossible to find white sandals at the end of August. "But madame, we're getting ready for back-to-school now." Finally she finds something not very attractive and one size too big.

She looks at her big little boy posing proudly in front of the mirrors at the store, with his wooden sword jammed into one of the belt loops of his Bermuda shorts, and his new shoes. For him they're intergalactic boots with laser buckles, beyond a shadow of a doubt. She thinks he's adorable with his hideous sandals.

Suddenly, she receives a good kick in the stomach. A kick from the inside.

She's felt jerks, jolts, and things inside but there, for the first time, it's plain and clear.

". . . Madame? Madame? . . . Will that be all? . . ."

"Yes, yes of course, excuse me."

"It's no problem, madame. You want a balloon, sweetie?"

On Sundays her husband putters around the house. He's fixing up a little bedroom in the space they used for a laundry room. Often, he asks his brother to lend him a hand. She bought beer and she's always scolding the little one so that he doesn't get underfoot.

Before going to bed she sometimes flips through decorating magazines to find ideas. Anyway, there's no rush.

They don't talk about the name because they don't really agree, and since they know very well that she'll have the last word . . . what's the point?

On Thursday, August 20, she has to go to the six-month exam. What a drag.

It's not very good timing, what with the wedding preparations. Especially since the bridal couple went to Rungis that same morning and brought back mountains of flowers. They requisitioned both bathtubs and the plastic kiddie pool for the occasion.

About two in the afternoon, she puts down her shears,

she takes off her apron, and she tells them that the little one's sleeping in the yellow bedroom. If he wakes up before she gets back, could you give him a snack? No, no, she won't forget to pick up bread, superglue, and raffia.

After taking a shower, she slides her big belly behind the wheel of her car.

She clicks on the radio and tells herself that in the end, it's not so bad, this break, because a bunch of women sitting around a table with their hands busy, they'll soon be telling a lot of tales. Big ones and little ones, too.

In the waiting room, there are already two other ladies. The big game in these cases is always to try to guess by the shape of their bellies what month they're in.

She reads a *Paris Match* from the time of Moses, when Johnny Hallyday was still with Adeline.

When she goes in, it's a handshake, you're doing all right? Yes, thanks, and you? She puts down her bag and sits. He plunks her name into the computer. He knows now how many weeks of gestation she's at and everything that follows.

Then she gets undressed. He rolls out some paper on the table while she weighs herself and then he's going to take her blood pressure. He's going to do a quick "check-up" ultrasound to see the heart. Once the exam's over, he'll go back to his computer to add a few things.

Gynecologists have a trick of their own. When the woman has propped her heels in the stirrups, they ask a multitude of questions out of the blue so that she'll forget, if only for a moment, about being in such an immodest position.

Sometimes it works, a little bit, more often not.

In this case, he asks her if she's felt it move; she begins to answer that before yes but now less often, but she doesn't finish her sentence because she sees clearly that he's not listening. Apparently he's already understood. He fiddles with the buttons of the machine to put her off the scent but he's already understood.

He places the monitor in another position but his movements are so brusque and his face is so old all of a sudden. She lifts herself on her forearms and she's understood too but she says: What's going on?

He tells her "Go get dressed" as if he hadn't heard her and she asks again: What's going on? He answers: there's a problem, the fetus isn't alive anymore.

She gets dressed.

When she comes back to sit down, she's silent and her face doesn't show anything. He types a bunch of stuff on his keyboard and at the same time he makes some phone calls.

He tells her: "We're about to spend some not-very-fun moments together."

At the moment, she doesn't know what to make of a statement like that.

By "some not-very-fun moments," maybe he meant the thousands of blood tests that would leave her arm a mess, or the ultrasound the next day, the images on the screen and all the measurements to understand what he would never understand. Unless "some not-very-fun moments" was the emergency delivery on Sunday night with the on-call doctor mildly annoyed to be woken up *again*.

Yes, that must be it, "some not-very-fun moments," that must be to give birth in pain and without anesthetic because it's too late. To be in so much pain that you throw up all over yourself instead of pushing like they tell you to. To see your husband powerless and so awkward as he caresses your hand and finally to push it out, this dead thing.

Then again, "some not-very-fun moments" is to be stretched out the next day in the maternity ward with an empty belly and the sound of a crying baby in the room next door.

The only thing that she won't be able to figure out is why he said "*we* are about to spend some not-very-fun moments . . ."

For now, he continues to fill out her file, and in between clicks he talks about having the fetus dissected and analyzed in Paris at the I-don't-know-what center but she hasn't been listening to him anymore for some time.

He tells her, "I admire your composure." She doesn't answer.

She goes out by the little door in back because she doesn't want to walk through the waiting room again.

She'll cry for a long time in her car but there's one thing she's sure of, she won't spoil the wedding. For the sake of the others, her grief can surely wait two days.

And that Saturday, she put on her linen dress with the little mother-of-pearl buttons.

She dressed her little boy and took his picture because she knows all too well that a getup like that, like a Little Lord Fauntleroy, won't last long.

Before going to the church they stopped at the clinic so that she could take, under close supervision, one of those awful pills that force all babies out, wanted or not.

She threw rice at the newlyweds and she walked down the well-raked gravel paths with a glass of champagne in her hand.

She raised her eyebrows when she saw her Little Lord Fauntleroy drinking soda straight from the bottle and she worried about the bouquets. She made small talk since it fit the time and the place.

And the other woman came up just like that, out of nowhere, a ravishing young woman she didn't know, from the groom's side, no doubt.

In an act of total spontaneity, she placed her hands flat on her belly and said: "May I? . . . They say it brings luck. . . ."

What did you want her to do? She tried to smile, of course.

This Man and This Woman

This man and this woman are in a foreign car. The car cost forty-nine thousand euros, but, strangely enough, what made the man hesitate back at the dealership was mainly the cost of the registration and taxes.

The wiper fluid doesn't shoot up right on the passenger side, and it's driving him crazy.

On Monday, he'll ask his secretary to call Salomon. For just a second he thinks about his secretary's breasts, which are very small. He's never slept with his secretaries. It's vulgar, and these days it could cost you some serious money. Anyway, he doesn't cheat on his wife anymore, not since the day he and Antoine Say entertained themselves during a round of golf by calculating just how much each of them would have to pay in alimony.

They're headed to their place in the country—a very pretty farmhouse, out near Angers. Great layout.

They bought it for next to nothing. The renovations, on the other hand . . .

There's paneling in every room, and a fireplace they'd had dismantled and then put back together, stone by stone, after they fell in love with it at an English antique shop. Every window's draped in heavy fabric, held in place with tiebacks. There's a totally modern kitchen, with damask dish towels and gray marble countertops . . . as many bathrooms as bedrooms . . . not much furniture, but all period pieces. On the walls are huge, gilded frames that overwhelm the nineteenth-century engravings they hold—mostly hunting scenes.

It's all kind of nouveau riche, but fortunately they don't realize it.

The man's in his weekend getup, old tweed pants and a sky-blue cashmere turtleneck (a gift from his wife for his fiftieth birthday). His shoes are John Lobbs—no way he'd ever change brands, not for the world. Obviously, his socks are made of lisle yarn and come up to his knees. Obviously.

He drives kind of fast, lost in thought. When he gets there, he'll have to talk to the caretakers about the property, the housework, pruning the beeches, poaching . . . and he hates all that.

He hates it when he feels like someone's taking him for a ride, and that's exactly what happens with those two, who start work Friday morning, dragging their feet, because they know the boss will be showing up that night, and they have to make it look like they've done something.

He ought to just get rid of them, but he really doesn't have the time to deal with it right now.

He's tired. His partners annoy the crap out of him, he almost never makes love to his wife anymore, his windshield is riddled with mosquitoes, and the wiper fluid doesn't shoot up right on the passenger side.

The woman's name is Mathilde. She's pretty, but in her face you can see all the things she's given up on in life.

She's always known when her husband was cheating on her, and she also knows that, if he doesn't do it anymore, it's the same old story—money.

She's in the dead man's seat. She's always very melancholy during these endless weekend drives to the country and back.

She thinks about how she's never been loved, she thinks

about how she never had any kids, she thinks about the caretaker's little boy, Kevin, who's going to be three in January. . . . Kevin, what a horrible name. If she'd had a son, she'd have named him Pierre, like her father. She remembers that awful scene when she mentioned adoption. . . . But she also thinks about the nice little green tailored suit she saw the other day in the window at Cerruti's.

They're listening to the radio station FIP. It's good, FIP: classical music that you can be proud of being able to appreciate, music from around the world that makes you feel like you're open-minded, and short little news briefs that barely leave enough time for the misery to come rushing into the car.

They've just passed the toll. They haven't exchanged a single word, and they still have a long way to go.

The Opel Touch

Just as you see me now, I'm walking down the rue Eugène-Gonon.

The whole deal.

What, no shit? You don't know the rue Eugène-Gonon? Hold on, are you kidding me?

The whole street's lined with these little millstone houses, with little lawns and forged iron marquees. The famous rue Eugène-Gonon in Melun.

Oh, come on! You know, *Melun* . . . the place with the prison, the brie—its brie deserves to be better known— and the train accidents.

Melun.

Sixth zone on the Paris-area transit pass.

I take the rue Eugène-Gonon several times a day. Four in all.

I go to class, I come back from class, I eat, I go to class, I come back from class.

At the end of the day, I'm wiped out.

I know it doesn't seem that bad, but *you* try it. Take the rue Eugène-Gonon in Melun four times a day to go to law school so you can take exams for ten years to prep for a career you don't even want. . . . Years and years of civil law, penal law, course packs, articles, paragraphs, legal texts, you name it. And mind you, all for a career that already bores me silly.

Be honest. Admit that I've got good reason to be wiped out at the end of the day.

So anyway, as I was saying, I'm on trip number three. I've had lunch and once again I'm setting off with a determined step toward the law school, yippee. I light a cigarette. All right, I say to myself, last one.

I start to snicker under my breath. If that's not the thousandth last one this year . . .

I walk along past the little millstone houses. *Villa Marie-Thérèse*, *My Felicity*, *Sweet Nest*. It's spring and I'm starting to get seriously depressed. Not the big guns: crocodile tears, medications, loss of appetite and all that crap. Nothing like that.

It's just . . . this trek down the rue Eugène-Gonon four

times a day. It wipes me out. Let those who are able to understand.

I don't see what that's got to do with the springtime. . . .

Yeah, well. In the spring, you've got little birds squabbling among the poplar buds. At night, tomcats making an infernal racket, drakes chasing after ducks on the Seine, plus all the lovers. Don't tell me you don't see them, the lovers, they're everywhere. Never-ending kisses with lots of saliva, hard-ons under jeans, roaming hands and every bench occupied. It drives me crazy.

It drives me crazy. That's all.

You're jealous? You hard up?

Me? Jealous? Hard up? Nononono, come on . . . you've gotta be kidding.

(. . .)

Hmpphh, whatever. That's all I need is to be jealous of these little jerks who grate on everybody's nerves with their lust. Whatever.

(. . .)

Hell, yes, I'm jealous!!! What, like it's not obvious? You need glasses? You don't see that I'm so jealous it's killing me, you don't see that I need loooovvve.

You can't see that? Yeah, well, I wonder what's wrong with you. . . .

I'm like a character out of a Brétécher comic strip: a girl seated on a bench with a sign around her neck: "I want love," and tears spouting like two fountains from either side of her eyes. I can see it now. What a sight.

Well, no, only now I'm not on rue Eugène-Gonon anymore (I have my dignity, after all), now I'm at Pramod.

Pramod's not hard to picture—they're everywhere. A department store, full of inexpensive clothes, mediocre quality . . . let's say passable, otherwise I might get fired.

It's my daily grind, my moola, my smokes, my espressos, my nights on the town, my good lingerie, my Guerlain, my blush splurges, my paperbacks, my flicks. Everything.

I hate working at Pramod, but without it? What would I do, wear stinking Gemey for ninety-five cents, rent movies at the Melun Video Club, and add the latest Jim Harrison in the suggestion book at the municipal library? No, thanks, I'd rather die. I'd rather work at Pramod.

And anyway, when I stop to think about it, I'd rather take on a bunch of pudgy women than the stench of the fryer at McDonald's.

The problem is my coworkers. I know what you're going to say: Girl, the problem is always the coworkers.

Okay, but do you know Marilyne Merchandise? (No kidding, she's the manager of the Pramod in downtown Melun and her name's Merchandise. . . . Oh, destiny.)

No, of course you don't know her, and yet she's the most, she's the most . . . managerial of managers of all the Pramods in France. And vulgar too, really vulgar.

I can't begin to tell you. It's not so much her looks, although . . . her dark roots and the cell phone on her hip kill me. . . . No, it's more a problem of the heart.

The vulgarity of the heart, that's an inexpressible thing.

Look there, how she speaks to her employees. It's crap. Her upper lip is curling, she must think we're sooo, sooo stupid. For me, it's worse, I'm the brain. The one who makes fewer spelling errors than she does, and that really pisses her off.

"Your going to love our new summer fashions!"

Hold on, hon . . . there's a problem.

No one ever taught you how to tell the difference between a possessive pronoun and a contraction? In your bleached little head you say to yourself, "I'm or he's or she's going to love our new summer fashions." See, it's not hard, you just put the noun and the verb together! Isn't that something!?

My, oh my, how she looks at me. Then she goes and re-does her sign:

"*You will* love our new summer fashions!" I gloat.

When she talks to me her lip stays in place, but it's killing her.

Note that aside from the energy spent managing my manager, I do all right.

I don't care what customer you give me, I'll dress her head to toe. Accessories included. Why? Because I look at her. Before I give her any advice, I look at her. I like looking at people. Especially women.

Even the ugliest ones, there's always something. At least the desire to be pretty.

"Marianne, I can't believe it, the summer bodysuits are still in the storeroom. You'd better go. . . ." You have to tell them everything, it's unbelievable. . . .

I'm going, I'm going. All the same.

I want love.

Saturday night, *zee Saturday night fever.*

The Milton is Melun's cowboy saloon; I'm with my girl-friends.

I'm glad they're here. They're pretty, they laugh a lot, and they know how to handle themselves.

I hear the screech of GTIs in the parking lot, the putt-ut-uh putt-ut-uh of undersized Harleys, and the click of Zippo lighters. Someone hands us cocktails on the house, but they're too sweet—they must have put in a ton of grenadine to keep down the costs on the good stuff. Plus, everyone knows, girls like grenadine. . . . But what the hell am I doing here? I'm a bundle of nerves. My eyes are stinging. Lucky me, I wear contacts, so with the smoke, go figure.

"Hi, Marianne, how are you?" asks a chick I knew in high school.

"Hi!" . . . *leaning forward for the four kisses* . . . "All right. Good to see you, it's been a while. . . . Where've you been?"

"You didn't hear? I was in the *States*. Get this, you'll never believe it, it was a hell of a deal. L.A., a mansion, you can't even imagine. Swimming pool, Jacuzzi, a super view of the ocean. And get this, the best part, it was with super-cool people, not the usual uptight Americans you see. God, no, it was too much."

She shakes her California highlights to show her immense nostalgia.

"You didn't run into George Clooney?"

"What . . . why do you ask?"

"No, no, never mind. I thought, to top it all off, you'd have met George Clooney, that's all."

"You're messed up, you know," she finishes, going off to romanticize her little au pair stint for the benefit of other, less candid souls.

Hey, look who's there . . . it's Buffalo Bill.

A skinny kid with a prominent Adam's apple and a little, meticulously maintained goatee—everything I go for— comes up to my breasts and tries to brush up against them.

The guy: "Don't we know each other from somewhere?"

My breasts: ". . ."

The guy: "Yes, of course! I remember now, weren't you at the Garage on Halloween?"

My breasts: ". . ."

The guy, not giving up: "Are you French?" And, in English, *"Do you understand me?"*

My breasts: ". . ."

Eventually, Buffalo raises his head. Oh, look, what do you know? . . . I have a face.

He scratches his goatee in sign of defeat (scritch scritch scritch) and seems plunged in deep thought.

"From where are you from?"

Wooowww, Buffalo! Vous parlez cowboy!

"From Melun, 4 Place de la Gare, and I might as well tell you right now, I haven't got a walkie-talkie stashed in my bra."

Scritch scritch . . .

I have to go. I can't see a thing anymore. Fuck these contacts.

Plus, you're crude, girl.

I'm in front of the Milton, I'm cold, I'm crying like a baby, I wish I were anywhere but here, I wonder how the hell I'm going to get back home. I look at the stars, and there aren't even any. So I cry even harder.

In cases like this, when the situation is this desperate, the smartest thing I can do . . . is call my sister.

Dring driiiinng driiinng . . .

"Hello . . ." (husky voice)

"Hey, it's Marianne."

"What time is it? Where are you?" (irritated voice)

"I'm at the Milton, can you come get me?"

"What happened? What's the matter?" (worried voice)

I repeat:

"Can you come get me?"

Headlights flash at the far end of the parking lot.

"Come on, hon, get in," says my sister.

"What's with the old-lady nightgown?!!"

"I came as fast as I could, I'll have you know."

"You came to the Milton in a see-through granny nightie!" I say, laughing my ass off.

"First off, I'm not getting out of the car like this, second, it's not see-through, it's openwork, didn't they teach you that at Pramod?"

"What if you run out of gas? Not to mention, some of your old admirers are here. . . ."

"No way . . . where?" (interested)

"Look, is that 'Teflon Pan' by any chance?"

"Move a little. . . . Oh, yeah! You're right. . . . God, he's ugly, he's even uglier than before. What's he driving these days?"

"An Opel."

"Oh! I see, 'The Opel Touch,' it's on the back windshield."

She looks at me, and we laugh like maniacs. We're together and we laugh:

1) at the good old days

2) at "Teflon Pan" (because above all he didn't want to get attached)

3) at his customized Opel

4) at his fleece-covered steering wheel

5) at the Perfecto motorcycle jacket that he only wears on the weekends and at the impeccable crease in his 501 jeans that his mom gets by bearing down really hard on the iron.

I feel better.

My sister, with her big yuppie car, peels out of the Milton parking lot. Heads turn. She says, "Jojo's gonna have a fit, that ruins the tires. . . ."

She laughs.

I take out my contacts and tilt the seat back.

We go in on tiptoe because Jojo and the kids are sleeping.

My sister pours me a gin and tonic, no Schweppes, and says:

"So what's up?"

So I tell her. But without getting my hopes up because my sister's not much of a psychologist.

I tell her that my heart is like a big empty sack. The sack's sturdy, it could hold a whole marketplace, and yet, there's nothing inside.

I say a sack, but I'm not talking about those pathetic little bags they have at the supermarket that always split open.

My sack . . . at least the way I picture it . . . it looks more like one of those big square white-and-blue-striped contraptions that the big black mamas carry on top of their heads in Paris in the Barbès district.

"Oh well . . . we're in deep now," my sister says as she pours us each another glass.

Amber

I've fucked thousands of girls and most of them, I don't even remember their faces.

I'm not saying that to be a smart-ass. At the point I'm at, with all the cash I'm making and all the ass kissers I've got hanging around, you really think I need to run my mouth just for the hell of it?

I'm saying it because it's true. I'm thirty-eight years old and I've forgotten just about everything that's happened in my life. It's true of the girls and it's true of everything else.

I happened to run across an old magazine the other day, the kind fit to wipe your ass with, and I saw a picture of me with some bimbette on my arm.

So I go read the caption and I learn that the girl in question is named Laetitia or Sonia or whatever, and I look at the picture again like that's gonna help, like I'll be able to say: "Oh, yeah, of course, Sonia, the little brunette from the Villa Barclay, the one with all the piercings and the vanilla-scented perfume. . . ."

But no. I can't remember any of it.

In my head I keep repeating "Sonia" like a jackass, and I put down the magazine to look for a cigarette.

I'm thirty-eight years old and I'm well aware that my life is going up in fucking smoke. The ceiling is flaking off oh-so-gently. One scratch of the fingernail and entire weeks are gone. Seriously, the other day I heard someone talking about the Gulf War. I turned around and said:

"When was that, the Gulf War?"

"In 'ninety-one," they answered, like I needed the *Britannica* for the details. . . . But the truth is, fuck it, that was the first time I'd heard anybody mention it.

The whole Gulf War, gone.

Never saw it. Never heard about it. A whole year that's now useless to me.

In 1991, I wasn't there.

In 1991, I was probably busy trying to find my veins and didn't notice there was a war. What the fuck, it doesn't matter. I'm talking about the Gulf War because it's a good example.

I forget just about everything.

Sorry, Sonia, but it's true. I don't remember you.

And then I met Amber.

All I have to do is say her name, and I feel good.

Amber.

The first time I saw her was at the recording studio on rue Guillaume Tell. We'd been up shit's creek all week and everyone was busting our balls about the money because we were late.

You can't plan for everything. It just can't be done. Take us: When we paid a small fortune to bring that hot-shot mixer over from the *States* to make all the fat cats at the record company happy, there's no way we could've known he was gonna croak on us on the first track.

"The strain and the jet lag must not have agreed with him," said the doctor.

Obviously, that was a load of shit, jet lag had nothing to do with it.

The jerk just had eyes that were bigger than his stomach, and so much the worse for him. Now he looked like an ass with his contract "to make the little *Frenchies* dance" . . .

That was a hellish time. I hadn't seen the light of day

for weeks and I didn't dare touch my hands to my face because it felt like my skin was going to crack or split open or something.

In the end I couldn't even smoke anymore because my throat was too sore.

Fred was annoying the shit out of me going on about some friend of his sister's. Some chick photographer who wanted to go along on tour with me—as a freelancer, but not to sell the photos. Just for herself.

"Hey, Fred, leave me alone about that. . . ."

"Wait, why would you give a fuck if I brought her here one night, huh? Why would you give a fuck?"

"I don't like photographers, or artistic directors, or journalists—I don't like people getting in my way, and I don't like people looking at me. You can understand that, can't you?"

"Shit, chill out. Just one night, two minutes. You won't even have to talk to her, chances are you won't even see her. Shit, do it for me. Obviously you don't know my sister."

Earlier I was telling you how I forget everything, but that, you see, no.

She came in through the little door that's on the right

when you're looking at the mixing station. She looked apologetic, walking on tiptoe, and she was wearing a white tank top with narrow straps. From where I was, be-hind the glass, I didn't see her face right away but when she sat down, I caught a glimpse of her small little breasts, and already I wanted to touch them.

Later she smiled at me. Not like the girls who usually smile at me, because they're happy to see that I'm looking at them.

She smiled at me to make me happy. And the take that day seemed to last forever.

When I finally got out of my glass cage, she was gone.

I asked Fred:

"That your sister's friend?"

"Yeah."

"What's her name?"

"Amber."

"She leave?"

"I dunno."

"Shit."

"What?"

"Nothing."

She came back on the last day. Paul Ackermann had

arranged a little party at the studio—"to celebrate your next gold disk," he'd said, that asshole. I was getting out of the shower—I was still bare-chested, rubbing my head with an oversized towel, when Fred introduced us.

I couldn't get a word out. It was like I was fifteen, and I let the towel drop to the floor.

She smiled at me again, just like before.

Picking up a bass, she asked:

"Is this your favorite guitar?"

And I couldn't figure out if the reason I wanted to kiss her was because she was so entirely clueless or because she was so goddamn polite.

Everyone else just says "hey, you" while cuffing me in the stomach. . . . From the president of the Republic down to the last asshole, all of them, they all act as if we'd raised pigs together.

It's the scene that does it.

"Yeah," I told her, "that's my favorite."

And I looked around for something to wear.

We talked for a while but it was hard because Ackermann had invited some journalists. I should've known.

She asked me about the tour and I said "yes" to everything she asked, looking at her breasts on the sly. Then she said good-bye and I looked everywhere for Fred, or Ackermann, or somebody, anybody. . . . I wanted to break somebody's neck because it was all boiling over inside.

There were ten dates to the tour, almost all of them outside France. We did two nights in Paris at the Cigale, and I get the rest all mixed up. We played Belgium, Germany, Canada, and Switzerland—but don't ask me in what order. I won't be able to give it to you.

Touring wears me out. I play my music, I sing, I try to stay *clean* (as much as I can), and I sleep in the Pullman.

Even if I start shitting gold I'll still go on the road with my band in an air-conditioned Pullman. The day you see me take a plane without them and then shake their hands just before we go onstage, you let me know because when that day comes, it means I don't give a shit about anything here anymore and it's time for me to move on.

Amber came with us but I didn't know it at first.

She took her photos without anyone even noticing. She roomed with the backup singers. You could hear them giggling in the hotel corridors sometimes when Jenny read their cards. Whenever I caught sight of her, I raised my head and tried to stand up straight. But in all those weeks, I never once went up to her.

I can't mix work and sex anymore. I'm too old.

The last night was a Sunday. We wanted to go out with a bang, so we were at Belfort doing a special concert for the tenth anniversary of Eurock Festival.

I sat down next to her at the farewell dinner.

It's like some kind of sacred thing . . . everyone respects it and keeps it just for us—the stage hands, the techies, the musicians, and everyone who helped us during the tour. It's not the time to let some starlet or small-time reporter give us shit, you know . . . even Ackermann wouldn't dare call Fred on his cell to get the latest update or to ask how many paid admissions we got.

I should probably mention that, in general, it's pretty bad for our image.

Among ourselves, we refer to these little parties as shroom fests, and that about says it all.

Tons of stress melting away, the satisfaction of a job well done, all those reels all snug in their cases, and my manager just beginning to smile for the first time in months . . . it's too much all at once, and it doesn't take much for it to get out of hand. . . .

At first I tried to get chatty with Amber, but then when I realized I was too far gone to fuck her decently, I let it go.

She didn't say a thing, but I know she knew exactly what was going on.

At one point, when I was in the can at the restaurant, I stood in front of the mirror by the sinks and said her name slowly. Instead of taking a good deep breath and splashing some cold water on my face and going to tell her to her face: "When I look at you, my gut aches like I'm in front of ten thousand people. . . . Please, make it stop . . . and just take me in your arms. . . ." No, instead of doing that, I turned around and got some from the dealer on duty, three hundred euros and I was gone.

Months went by, the album came out . . . I won't tell you any more about it. It's a period I handle worse and worse . . . when I can't be alone anymore with my point-less questions and music.

As usual, Fred was the one who took me to her. He picked me up on his black Vmax.

She wanted to show us her work from the tour.

I was feeling good. I was glad to see Vickie, Nat, and Francesca again—they all used to sing live with me. They were all going their separate ways now, every one of them. Francesca wanted to do a solo album, so I got down on my knees and promised her, one more time, to write her something unforgettable.

Her apartment was miniscule and we were all tripping over each other. We drank some sort of pink tequila that the neighbor down the hall had scrounged up. He was Argentinean, at least six foot six, and he smiled all the time.

I was dumbfounded by his tattoos.

I got up. I knew she was in the kitchen. She asked:

"You've come to help me?"

I said no.

She asked:

"You want to see my photos?"

I wanted to say no again, but I said:

"Yeah, I'd like that."

She went into her room. When she came back, she locked the door and cleared everything off the table with a sweep of her arm. It made quite a racket, thanks to some aluminum trays.

She set her box of pictures down flat, and she sat down across from me.

I opened it. All I saw were my hands.

Hundreds of black-and-white photos of nothing but my hands.

My hands on guitar strings, my hands around the mike, my hands beside my body, my hands caressing the crowd, my hands shaking other hands backstage, my hands holding a cigarette, my hands touching my face, my hands signing autographs, my hands feverish, my hands beseeching, my hands throwing kisses, and my hands shooting up, too.

Big, thin hands with veins like little rivers.

Amber was toying with a bottle cap, crushing crumbs.

"That's it?" I said.

For the first time, I looked her in the eyes for more than a second.

"You disappointed?"

"I don't know."

"I took your hands because that's the only thing about you that's not falling apart."

"You think so?"

She nodded her head yes and I caught the scent of her hair.

"What about my heart?"

She smiled at me and leaned across the table.

"You're telling me your heart's not falling apart?" she answered with a doubting little pout.

We heard laughter and tapping on the other side of the door. I recognized Luis's voice shrieking: *"We need i-eece!"*

I said:

"I don't know, have to see. . . ."

I thought they were going to break down the door with the shit they were pulling.

She put her hands on mine and looked at them like she was seeing them for the first time. She said:

"That's exactly what we're going to do."

Leave

Whenever I do anything, I think of my brother, and whenever I think of my brother, I realize he'd have done it better than me.

Twenty-three years this has been going on.

You can't really say that makes me bitter; no, it just makes me lucid.

Now, for instance, I'm on train #1458 from Nancy, in northeastern France. I'm on leave—my first in three months.

Okay, for starters, I'm doing my military service like some measly errand boy, whereas my brother went through officer training. He always ate at the officers' table, and he got to come home every weekend. Let's move on.

I'm coming back by train. I've reserved a seat facing forward, but when I get there, there's some lady sitting there with a whole jumble of embroidery spread out over her knees. I don't dare say anything. I swing my huge canvas bag up onto the luggage rack and sit down across from her. There's a girl in the same car who's kind of pretty, reading the latest Jackie Collins. She's got a zit at the corner of her lip. Too bad; otherwise she's decent.

I go buy myself a sandwich from the dining car.

And here's how that would have worked if it had been my brother: He'd have flashed the lady a big charming smile and shown her his ticket with an *excuse me, madame, listen, I may have made a mistake but it seems to me . . .* And she'd have apologized like crazy, stuffing all her pieces of thread in her bag and getting up in a hurry.

For the sandwich, he'd have made some kind of scene with the guy, saying that for four euros, really, they could at least give him a little thicker slice of ham. And the waiter, with his ridiculous black vest, would've changed the sandwich pronto. I should know, I've seen my brother in action.

As for the girl, it's even more messed up. He'd have given her one of those looks so she'd have known right away he was interested.

But she'd have known at exactly the same time that he'd also noticed her little pimple. And then she'd have had a hard time concentrating on her novel, and she'd try to play it cool just in case.

That is, if he intended to take an interest in her.

Because, anyway, junior officers ride in first class, and how many girls in first have zits?

As for me, I never even found out if this chick was impressed with my crew cut and ranger boots, because I fell asleep almost right away. They'd dragged us out of bed at four again this morning to make us do some bone-headed drill.

Marc, my brother, did his stint in the military after three years of prep school, before he started his engineering studies. He was twenty.

Me, I'm doing it after two years of vocational training, and when I finish I'll be looking for a job in electronics. I'm twenty-three.

What's more, tomorrow's my birthday.

My mother insisted that I come home. I'm not real big on birthdays—I'm too old for that. But whatever. I'm doing it for her.

She's lived alone ever since my father ran off with the neighbor lady on their nineteenth anniversary. Symbolically, you could say, it was rich.

I don't really understand why she hasn't started over with someone else. She could have—actually, she still could, but . . . I don't know. Marc and I only talked about it just one time and we agreed: we think she's afraid now. She doesn't want to risk being abandoned all over again. At one point, we tried to coax her into signing up for one of those matchmaking things, but she never wanted to.

Since then, she's taken in two dogs and a cat, so you can imagine . . . with a menagerie like that, finding a nice guy is pretty much Mission Impossible.

We live just south of Paris, near the suburb of Corbeil, in a little villa on Highway 7. It's okay. It's quiet.

My brother never says *villa*, he says *house*. He thinks the word *villa* is hick.

My brother will never get over the fact that he wasn't born in Paris.

Paris. It's all he ever talks about. I think the best day of his life was when he bought his first mass transit pass so he could go into the city. For me—Paris, Corbeil—it's all the same.

One of the few things I remember from school is a theory by one of those ancient philosophers, who said the important thing isn't where you are, it's the state of mind you're in.

I remember he wrote that to one of his friends who was feeling down and was thinking about hitting the road. He basically told him, in so many words, that it wasn't worth the trouble since he was bound to lug his load of problems around wherever he went. The day the teacher told us that, my life changed.

That's one of the reasons I picked a career in manual labor.

I'd rather let my hands do the thinking. It's easier.

In the army, you meet your fair share of morons. I live with guys I never could've imagined. I bunk with them, get dressed with them, eat with them, clown around with them, sometimes even play cards with them . . . but still, it's like everything about them makes me sick. I'm not a snob or anything, it's just that these guys have zilch. And I'm not talking about being deep or whatever—that's like some kind of insult. I'm talking about weighing something.

I know I'm not doing a very good job explaining myself, but I know what I mean. If you took one of these guys and put him on a scale, obviously you'd have his weight, but really, he doesn't weigh anything. . . .

It's like there's nothing in these guys that has any real substance. They're like ghosts—you can stick your arm right through them and all you'll touch is a big, noisy void. Of course, if you tell them that, they'll say if you try to stick your arm through, you're asking for it. Har har.

At first, I couldn't sleep at night because of all the crap they pulled and all the crazy shit they'd say. But now I'm used to it. They say the army makes a man of you, but in my case it's only made me even more pessimistic.

I'm not inclined to believe in God or some Superior Thing, because it's hard to imagine that anyone could have purposely created what I see every day in the barracks at Nancy-Bellefond.

It's funny, I do more thinking when I'm on the train . . . like why the army's not all bad. . . .

When I get to the Paris station, Gare de l'Est, I always secretly hope there'll be someone waiting for me. It's stupid. I already know my mom's at work, and Marc's not the kind of guy to come slogging across the suburbs just so he can carry my bag. But still, I always have this idiotic hope.

This time's no different. Before I take the escalator down to the metro, I take a quick look around, just in case there's anyone there. . . . And when I get on the escalator, my bag seems a little heavier, same as always.

I wish someone were waiting for me somewhere. . . . Is that so much to ask?

Fine, whatever. It's time for me to get to the house. I

could use a good scuffle with Marc—I'm starting to think too much and I'm about to blow a gasket. While I'm waiting for the train, I'm gonna have a smoke on the platform. I know it's against the rules, but just let them mess with me—I'll pull the military card.

I work for Peace, monsieur! I get up at four in the morning for France, madame.

No one at the station in Corbeil . . . that's a little harder to take. Maybe they forgot I was coming tonight. . . .

I'll walk the rest of the way. I'm sick of communal transportation. In fact, I think I'm sick of everything communal.

I run into some guys I went to school with. They're in no big hurry to shake my hand. Face it, the army sucks.

I stop in at the café on the corner of my street. If I'd spent less time in this café growing up, maybe now I wouldn't be in danger of having to go down to the unemployment agency in another six months. There was a time when I used to spend more time behind this pinball machine than in the classroom . . . I'd play until five o'clock, and then when the other kids showed up, the ones who'd had to listen to the teachers' blabbering all day, I'd sell them my bonus rounds. It was a good deal for them: they paid half price and had a chance to get their initials on the high score list.

Everyone was happy, and I bought myself my first packs of smokes. I swear, back then, I thought I was king. The king of jerks, maybe.

The owner says:

"So? . . . Still in the army?"

"Yeah."

"Good for you!"

"Yeah . . ."

"So come see me some night after I close, so we can chat. . . . You know, I was in the Legion myself, and that was really somethin' else. . . . They'd never have let us take a weekend off just like that, I can tell you."

And he goes back to the counter to relive the war with his drunken cronies.

The Legion . . .

I'm tired. I'm fed up with this bag cutting into my shoulder and the street just keeps on going. When I get to my house, the gate is locked. Fuck, that does it. I could just about cry right there.

I've been on my feet since four a.m., I've just come halfway across the country in stinking train cars, and now it's about time to cut me some slack, don't you think?

The dogs are waiting for me. Between Bozo howling himself to death for joy and Micmac jumping ten feet in the air . . . it's a party. Now *that's* a welcome.

I throw my bag over the top and go over the wall like I used to back in my moped-riding days. The dogs pounce on me, and for the first time in weeks, I feel better. So there, there are still living creatures on this little planet who love me and are happy to see me. Come here, my sweet things. Oh, yes, you're beautiful, you, oh, yes, you're beautiful!

The house is dark.

I put my bag down on the doormat by my feet. I open it and start hunting for my keys, which are all the way at the bottom under tons of dirty socks.

The dogs go in ahead of me and I go to turn on the hall light . . . no power.

Well, shiiiiiiit. Well, shit.

Just then I hear Marc, that butt-fuck, saying:

"Hey, show some manners in front of your guests."

It's still dark. I answer:

"What is this shit?"

"Aren't you a delinquent second-class grunt. Enough of the four-letter words. We're not in the Hickville barracks here, so watch your mouth or I won't turn on the lights."

He turns the lights on.

That's all I need: All my friends and my whole family

are there in the living room, holding on to their drinks and standing around under paper garlands, singing "Happy Birthday."

My mother says:

"Well, kiddo, put down your bag."

And she hands me a drink.

No one's ever done anything like this for me before. I can't be looking all that great, standing there with a stupid look on my face.

I go shake everyone's hand and kiss my grandmother and my aunts.

When I get to Marc, I mean to slap him upside the head, but he's with a girl. He's got his arm around her waist. And from the minute I see her, I already know I'm in love.

I give my brother a punch on the shoulder, and, jerking my chin at the girl, I ask:

"That my present?"

"Dream on, moron," he answers.

I'm still looking at her. It's like there's something playing the clown in my stomach. I feel sick, and she's beautiful.

"You don't recognize her?"

"No."

"Of course you do, it's Marie, Rebecca's friend. . . ."

"???"

She says:

"We went to summer camp together. At Glénans, don't you remember? . . ."

"Nope, sorry." I shake my head and ditch them. I go get myself something to drink.

Damn right, I remember her. I still have nightmares about that sailing course. My brother, always first. He was the counselors' pet: tan, muscular, laid-back. He read an instruction manual at night, and he understood everything as soon as he got on board. I can still see him going out on the trapeze and sending up a spray of water, yelling over the waves. He never capsized once.

All those girls with their little breasts and their vacant eyes staring like fish on a platter, thinking of nothing but the party on the last night.

All those girls who'd written their addresses on his arm with a felt-tip pen while he was pretending to sleep on the bus. And the ones who cried in front of their parents when they saw him heading toward our family Renault.

And me . . . getting seasick.

Yeah, I remember Marie, all right. One night, she was telling some of the other kids that she'd surprised a cou-

ple of lovers kissing on the beach, and that she'd heard the
sound of the girl's panties snapping.

"What did it sound like?" I asked, just to put her on
the spot.

She looked me straight in the eye. She pinched her un-
derwear through the cloth of her dress, pulled it back, and
let it go.

Snap.

"Like that," she answered, still looking at me.

I was eleven.

Marie.

Damn right, I remember. Snap.

The later it got, the less I felt like talking about the
army. The less I looked at Marie, the more I wanted to
touch her.

I drank too much. My mother shot me a dirty look.

I went out in the garden with a couple of friends from
tech school. We were talking about videos we wanted to
rent and cars we'd never be able to buy. Michael had put
a hyped-up sound system in his Peugeot.

Almost two thousand francs to listen to techno. . . .

I sat down on the iron bench—the one my mother
asks me to repaint every year. She says it reminds her of
the Tuileries garden in Paris.

I smoked a cigarette, looking at the stars. I don't know

many by name. So whenever I have a chance, I look for them. I know four.

Another lesson from Glénans that didn't quite take.

I saw her coming while she was still a ways off. She smiled at me. I looked at her teeth and the shape of her earrings.

She sat down next to me and said:

"May I?"

I didn't answer because my stomach was hurting again.

"So, is it true you don't remember me?"

"No, it's not."

"You do remember?"

"Yes."

"What do you remember?"

"I remember that you were ten, that you were four foot three, that you weighed fifty-seven pounds and that you'd had the mumps the year before. I remember the medical exam. I remember that you lived at Choisy-le-Roi and at the time it would have cost me forty-two francs to go see you by train. I remember that your mother's name was Catherine and your father's name was Jacques. I remember that you had a water turtle named Candy, and your best friend was a guinea pig named Anthony. I remember that you had a green bathing suit with white stars, and your mother had even made you a robe with your name embroidered on it. I remember that you cried one morning because you didn't have any mail. I remember that you stuck some sequins on your cheeks the night of the party, and you and Rebecca put on a show to the music from *Grease*. . . ."

"Oh la la—it's incredible that you remember those things!!"

She's even more beautiful when she laughs. She leans back and rubs her hands on her arms to warm them up.

"Here," I say, pulling off my sweater.

"Thanks . . . but what about you? Aren't you going to be cold?!"

"Don't worry about me—go ahead."

She looks at me differently. Any girl would've understood what she understood just then.

"What else do you remember?"

"I remember that one night in front of the Optimists' shed you told me you thought my brother was a show-off. . . ."

"Yeah, that's right! I said that, and you told me it wasn't true."

"Because it's not. Marc does a million things like it's nothing, but he doesn't show off. He just does them, that's all."

"You always stuck up for your brother."

"Yeah, he's my brother. Besides, you don't think he's got all that many faults right now, either, do you?"

She got up. She asked if she could keep my sweater.

I smiled at her. Despite the bog of muck and misery I was flailing around in, I was happy as ever.

My mother came up while I was still smiling like a big, fat fool. She said she was going to sleep at my grand-mother's. The girls should sleep on the first floor and the boys on the second. . . .

"All right, Mom, we're not kids anymore, it's okay. . . ."

"And make sure the dogs are in before you lock up, and . . ."

"All right, Mom. . . ."

"I have a right to worry, you all drink like fish and you, you must be completely drunk. . . ."

"You don't say drunk in this case, Mom, you say 'wasted.' See, I'm wasted. . . ."

She backed off, shrugging her shoulders.

"At least put something on—you'll catch your death."

I smoked three more cigarettes, to give myself time to think, and then I went to find Marc.

"Hey . . ."

"What?"

"It's about Marie. . . ."

"What?"

"Let me have her."

"No."

"I'm gonna break your face."

"No."

"Why not?"

"Because you've had too much to drink tonight, and because I need to have my little angel face for work on Monday."

"Why?"

"Because I'm giving a talk on the incidence of fluids in an established area."

"Oh?"

"Yeah."

"Sorry."

"Don't mention it."

"And about Marie?"

"Marie? She's mine."

"Don't be so sure."

"What do you know about it?"

"Oh! It . . . Call it an artillery soldier's sixth sense."

"My ass it is."

"Listen, I'm up against a wall here—there's nothing I can do. That's just the way it is. I know, I'm an idiot. So let's find a solution at least for tonight, okay?"

"Let me think. . . ."

"Hurry up. Later I'll be too far gone."

"Foosball."

"What?"

"We'll play foosball for her."

"That's not very chivalrous."

"It'll be just between us, mister gentleman-ass-wipe who tries to steal other guys' girls."

"Okay. When?"

"Now. In the basement."

"Now??!"

"Yes, sir."

"I'll be right there. I'm going to make myself a mug of coffee."

"Make me one, too, please."

"No problem. I'll even piss in it."

"Military moron."

"Go warm up. Go tell her good-bye."

"Die."

"It's no big deal, go ahead. I'll console her."

"Count on it."

We drank our burning-hot coffees over the sink. Marc went downstairs first. Meanwhile, I stuck both my hands in a sack of flour. I thought about my mom making us breaded chicken.

Only now I had to piss. Wasn't that brilliant. Holding

on to it with two chicken cordon bleus . . . it's not the most practical thing. . . .

Before I went down, I looked around for Marie. I needed to buck up my resolve, because if I'm a pinball-playing fiend, foosball's more my brother's thing.

I played like shit. The flour was supposed to keep me from sweating, but instead it just turned the tips of my fingers into little white meatballs.

Plus, Marie and the others came down when we were 6 even, and from then on, I lost it. I could feel her moving behind me, and my hands slipped on the handles. I smelled her perfume and forgot my attackers. I heard the sound of her voice, and I got slammed, goal after goal.

When my brother had moved the marker to 10 on his side, finally I could wipe my hands on my thighs. My jeans were all white.

Marc, the bastard, looked at me like he was really sorry. *Happy birthday,* I thought.

The girls said they wanted to go to bed and asked to be shown to their room. I said I was going to sleep on the couch in the living room so I could finish off the dregs of the bottle in peace, without anyone bothering me.

Marie looked at me. I thought that if only she were still four foot three inches tall and fifty-seven pounds right then, I could've tucked her inside my shirt and taken her with me everywhere.

And then the house got quiet. The lights went out, one after another, and I didn't hear anything except a few chuckles here and there.

I supposed Marc and his friends were acting like imbeciles, scratching at the girls' door.

I whistled for the dogs and locked the front door.

I couldn't fall asleep. Of course.

I smoked a cigarette in the dark. The only thing visible in the room was the little red point, moving a little from time to time. And then I heard a noise—like paper rustling. At first, I thought it was one of the dogs getting into trouble. I called:

"Bozo? . . . Micmac? . . ."

No response, and the noise was getting louder—now also with a scritch, scritch, like Scotch tape being pulled off.

I sat up and reached out to switch on the light.

I'm dreaming. Marie is standing in the middle of the room, naked, in the process of covering her body with pieces of wrapping paper. She has blue paper on her left breast, silver on the right, and ribbon twisted around her arms. There's some heavy paper that my grandmother had used to wrap the motorcycle helmet she gave me—she's got that wrapped around her like some kind of loincloth.

She's walking around half naked in the middle of all

the thrown-away wrappers, among the full ashtrays and the dirty glasses.

"What are you doing?"

"It's not obvious?"

"Well, no . . . not really. . . ."

"Didn't you say earlier, when you first got here, you wanted a present?"

She kept smiling and tied some red ribbon around her waist.

I got up right away.

"Hey, don't get too wrapped up," I said.

Even as I said it, I wondered if "don't get too wrapped up" meant: don't cover your skin like that—leave it for me, I beg you.

Or if "don't get too wrapped up" meant: don't invest too much too fast, you know . . . not only do I still get seasick, but on top of that, I've gotta go back to Nancy tomorrow, to the base, so, you see . . .

Lead Story

I'd be better off just going to bed, but I can't.

My hands are shaking.

Maybe I should write some sort of report.

I'm used to it. I write one every Friday afternoon for my boss, Guillemin.

This time I'll do it for myself.

I tell myself: "If you retell the whole thing just the way it happened, if you really apply yourself, then afterward when you read it back over, maybe, just maybe, for two seconds you'll be able to believe that dumbass in the story is someone else. And then maybe you'll be able to judge yourself objectively. Maybe."

So here I am. I'm sitting in front of the little laptop I

usually use for work. I hear the noise of the dishwasher downstairs.

My wife and kids went to bed a long time ago. I know the kids must be asleep, but I'm sure my wife's not. She's waiting up for me, trying to make sense of it all. I think she's afraid because she already knows she's lost me. Women can sense those things. But I can't just go curl up with her and fall asleep—and she knows that as well as I do. I need to write it all down for the sake of the two seconds that could be so important if I can just pull it off.

I'll start at the beginning.

I was hired at Paul Pridault on September 1, 1995. Before that I was with a competitor, but there were too many little things getting under my skin—like when the expense forms got paid six months late. So I packed it all in on a sudden whim.

I was out of work for almost a year.

Everyone thought I'd go nuts, sitting at home twiddling my thumbs and waiting for a call from the temp agency I'd signed up with.

But actually, I have a lot of good memories from that time. I was finally able to finish the house—all those things that Florence had been after me forever to get done. I hung all the curtain rods and fixed up a shower in the back storage room. I rented a rototiller, turned over the whole yard, and put down fresh sod.

In the afternoons, I'd go pick up Lucas from the sitter's, and then when school got out we'd go get his big sister. I'd fix them huge snacks and hot chocolate. Not Nesquik—real stirred cocoa that gave them great big mustaches. Afterward, we'd go look at them in the bathroom mirror before they licked them off.

In June, it dawned on me that Lucas wouldn't be going to Madame Ledoux's much longer, now that he was old enough for preschool. I started getting serious again about looking for work, and in August, I found it.

At Paul Pridault, I'm the sales rep for the whole western part of France. The company's a major pork producer—like a butcher, sort of, but on an industrial scale.

Old man Pridault's stroke of genius is his *jambon au torchon,* country ham wrapped in a real red-and-white-checked cloth. Of course, it's a factory ham made from factory pigs, and the famous country cloth is made in China, but whatever—it's what he's famous for. Just ask any housewife behind her shopping cart what the name Paul Pridault means to her, and she'll tell you *"jambon au torchon"*—all the market studies prove it. And if you press the point, you'll learn that our *jambon au torchon* is miles better than anybody else's because it tastes more authentic.

Hats off to the *artiste.*

We do a net annual revenue of five million euros.

I spend the better part of the week behind the wheel of my company car. A black Peugeot 306 with a grinning pig's head decaled on the sides.

People have no concept of what life's like for these guys on the road, all the truck drivers and sales reps.

It's like there are two worlds on the highway: those out for a drive, and us.

It's a bunch of things. First, there's the way we feel about our cars.

From the little Renault Clio to the big-ass German semis, when we climb in, we're at home. It's our smell, our mess, our seats taking the form of our asses—and believe me, we get enough shit about that. Then there's the CB, which is a whole mysterious world of its own, with codes most people can't even understand. I don't use it much. I put it on mute from time to time when I smell something burning, but that's all.

Then there's the whole food thing. The Cheval Blanc hotel-restaurants, the roadside diners, the ads for the golden arches. . . . Daily specials, pitchers, paper napkins. . . . All those faces that you pass and never see again. . . .

And the waitresses' asses—which are catalogued, rated, and updated better than the Michelin Guide. They call it the Micheline Guide.

There's the tiredness, the travel plans, the loneliness, the thoughts—always the same ones turning over and over.

Potbellies have a way of sneaking up on you. Hookers, too.

There's a whole universe that's like a big, insurmountable barrier between those who live on the road and those who don't.

Roughly speaking, my job consists of making the rounds to all our distribution outlets.

I work with mid- to large-scale grocery managers. We define launching strategies together, do sales projections, and conduct informational meetings about our products.

For me, it's a little like going for a walk with a pretty girl, showing everyone how sweet and charming she is. Like I'm trying to find her a good match.

But it doesn't end with finding her a husband—I still have to look out for her. When I get a chance, I test the vendors to see if they're putting our merchandise up front, if they're trying to sell generic stuff, if they've got the *torchon* cloth unfolded just like on TV, if the miniandouilles are bathing in their jelly, if the pâtés are in real old-fashioned terrines, if the sausages are hung up like they're drying, and if and if and if . . .

No one notices all these little details, but they're what make the Paul Pridault difference.

I know I'm talking too much about my work, and that has nothing to do with what I need to write.

Right now it's pork, but I could sell lipstick or shoe-laces just as well. What I love is making contacts, talking to people, and getting to see the country. Most of all, I love not being closed up in some office with a boss on my back all day. Just thinking about it puts me in anguish.

On Monday, September 29, 1997, I got up at a quarter to six. I got my stuff together without making a sound so my wife wouldn't grump at me. Then I barely had time to shower, because the car was almost out of gas and I wanted to use the chance to check the tire pressure.

I drank my coffee at the Shell station. I hate when I have to do that. The smell of diesel and sweetened coffee mixing together always makes me sort of want to throw up.

My first appointment was at eight-thirty at Pont-Audemer. I helped the shelf stockers at Carrefour, a big grocery chain, put together a new display shelf for our vacuum-packed meals. It's a new thing that just brought out in conjunction with a big-name chef. (You should see the profits he rakes in just for showing his pretty face and toque on the package, jeez.)

The second appointment was set for ten o'clock in the Bourg-Achard industrial zone.

I was running a little late, mostly due to fog on the highway.

I turned off the radio because I needed to think.

I was worried about this interview. I knew we were up against an important competitor, and it was a major challenge for me. Besides, I nearly missed my exit.

At one in the afternoon, I got a panicked phone call from my wife:

"Jean-Pierre, is that you?"

"What, who did you expect?"

". . . My God. . . . Are you okay?"

"Why are you asking me that?"

"Because of the accident, of course! For two hours I've been trying to reach you on your cell, but they said all the lines were overloaded! For two hours I've been sick with worry! I must've called your office at least ten times! Shit! You could at least have called, you know. You really suck. . . ."

"Wait, what are you talking about . . . what's this all about?"

"The accident this morning on Highway A13. Weren't you supposed to take the A13 today?"

"What accident?"

"You can't be serious!!! *You're* the one who listens to France Info all day!!! It's all anybody's talking about. Even on TV! There was a terrible accident this morning near Rouen."

". . ."

"Well, okay, I'll let you go, I've got a ton of work. . . . I haven't done a thing since this morning. I was sure I must be a widow. I could already see myself throwing a handful of dirt on your coffin. Your mother called, my mother called. . . . Talk about a morning."

"Nope! Sorry . . . not this time! You'll have to wait a little longer to get rid of my mother."

"Idiot."

". . ."

". . ."

"Hey, Flo . . ."

"What?"

"I love you."

"You never say it."

"And just now? What did I just do?"

". . . All right. . . . See you tonight. Call your mother or else she's the one who's gonna kick the bucket."

At seven o'clock I watched the local news. Awful.

Eight dead and sixty injured.

Cars crushed like cans.

How many?

Fifty? A hundred?

Trucks flattened and completely burned. Dozens and dozens of ambulances. A policeman talking about carelessness, about excessive speeding, about the fog that had been forecasted the night before, and about some bodies they still hadn't been able to identify. Haggard, silent people in tears.

At eight I listened to the news highlights on TV. Nine deaths this time.

Florence shouted from the kitchen:

"Enough already! Turn that off! Come in here."

We clinked glasses in the kitchen. But it was just to make her happy—my heart wasn't in it.

Right then, at that moment, I felt afraid. I couldn't eat anything, and I was stunned like a boxer who's been hit a few too many times.

Since I couldn't sleep, my wife made love to me, very gently.

At midnight I was back in the living room. I turned on

the TV and put it on mute, and I looked all over for a cigarette.

At twelve-thirty, I turned the volume back up a little to watch the last newscast. I couldn't tear my eyes from the mass of sheet metal scattered across the lanes in both directions.

What a fucked-up situation.

I said to myself: people are just way too stupid.

And then a truck driver came on the screen. He was wearing a T-shirt that said Le Castellet. I'll never forget his face.

That night, in my living room, this guy said:

"Okay, yeah, so it was foggy, and yeah, people drive too fast, but none of this shit ever would've happened if that dumb-shit hadn't backed up to make the Bourg-Achard exit. From the cab, I could see the whole thing. The two cars next to me slowed down, and then after that I could hear the others smooshing in like butter in a mold. Believe it or not, I couldn't see a thing in my mirrors. Nothing. It was all just white. I hope it doesn't keep you up at night, you bastard."

That's what he said. To me.

To me, Jean-Pierre Faret, butt-naked in my living room.

That was yesterday.

Today, I bought all the papers. On page 3 of the *Figaro* dated Tuesday, September 30:

DRIVER ERROR SUSPECTED

"An unlawful maneuver by a driver, who is thought to have backed up at the Bourg-Achard interchange in Eure, may have triggered the pileup that caused the deaths of nine persons yesterday morning in a series of collisions on Highway A13. The error is thought to have provoked the first collision, in the Paris-bound lanes, whereupon a tanker immediately caught fire. The flames attracted the attention of . . ."

And on page 3 of the *Parisien*:

THE SHOCKING THEORY OF A DRIVER ERROR

"The carelessness, indeed the recklessness, of a motorist may have been the source of the tragedy that manifested itself in the indescribable heap of crushed metal from which at least nine bodies were removed yesterday morning on Highway A13. Indeed, according to the shocking testimony taken down by police, a car backed up to make the Bourg-Achard exit, roughly twenty kilometers from Rouen. It was in an attempt to avoid this car that the . . ."

And as if that weren't enough:

"In trying to cross the highway in order to aid the injured, two other persons were killed, mowed down by a
car. In less than two minutes, roughly a hundred cars,
three semis . . ." (*Libération*, same day.)

Not even twenty meters, hardly—just a little shortcut
across the white stripes.
    It took a matter of seconds. I'd already forgotten.
    My God . . .
    I don't cry.

Florence came looking for me in the living room at five
in the morning.
    I told her everything, of course.

For several long minutes she stayed seated, without moving, her hands on her face.
    She looked to the right, then to the left, like she
needed air. Then she said:
    "Listen to me. Don't say anything. You know if you do
they'll charge you with involuntary manslaughter, and
you'll go to jail."

"Yes."

"And then? And then? What will that change? Even more lives fucked up, and how does that make it any better?"

She was crying.

"Well, there you have it. My life's already fucked."

She was shouting.

"Well, yours maybe, but not the kids'! So don't you say a thing!"

I didn't have the strength to shout.

"Let's talk about the kids. Look at that one. Take a good look at him."

And I held out the newspaper, on the page that showed a little boy in tears on Highway A13.

A little boy walking away from an unrecognizable car.

A photo in the paper.

In the section "Lead Story."

". . . He's the same age as Camille."

"Knock it off, stop that!" My wife was shrieking, grabbing me by the shirt collar. . . . "Stop that shit! You shut up, now! Let me ask you a question. Just one. What good does it do for a guy like you to go to jail? Huh? Tell me, what good will it do?!"

"It might make them feel better."

She walked away, crushed.

I heard her shut herself in the bathroom.

When I saw her this morning, I nodded. But now, tonight, in my silent house with just the background noise of the dishwasher . . .

I'm lost.

I'm going to go downstairs. I'm going to drink a glass of water and I'm going to smoke a cigarette in the garden. Then I'm going to come back up here and reread everything from start to finish. Maybe that will help.

But I don't think so.

Catgut

In the beginning, none of it was supposed to work out this way. I'd answered an ad in *Veterinary Week* to fill in for someone for two months, August and September. And then the guy who'd hired me was killed on the road on his way back from vacation. Fortunately, no one else was in the car.

So I stayed on and took over the practice. It has a good clientele. People in Normandy have a hard time paying, but eventually they pay.

People up there are like all rustics—once an idea gets ingrained . . . And a woman for the animals—that can't be good. To feed them, okay, and to milk them and clean up their shit, fine. But when it comes to things like shots, calving, colic, and metritis, they'll have to see. . . .

They saw. They spent several months checking me out before anyone finally invited me in for a drink.

Of course, in the mornings, it's no big deal—that's when I do consultations at the office. Mostly people bring in cats and dogs. I have all kinds of cases. Sometimes they'll bring one in for me to put down, because the father can't bring himself to do it and the animal's in pain . . . or they'll bring me one to treat, because "this one's a real good hunter" . . . and every now and then they'll bring one in for vaccinations—but in that case, the owner's always Parisian.

The hard part, at first, was the afternoons. The house calls. The cowsheds. The silences. *Hafta see 'er at work, then we'll see.* Nothing but mistrust—and, I can imagine, nothing but ridicule behind my back. Yeah, I must've really given them something to laugh about at the cafés, what with my lab work and my sterile gloves. Plus, my last name is Sirloine. Doctor Sirloine. What a joke.

In the end, I had to forget all the theoretical stuff we'd learned in school. I'd stand there silently in front of the livestock, waiting for the owner to spit out some scraps of information to help me figure out what was going on.

And then, most important—and this is the reason I've lasted this long—I bought myself some weights.

Now, if I had to give one piece of advice to a young

person who wanted to go rural (although after everything that's happened, I'd be surprised if anyone asked),
here's what I'd say: Muscles. Lots of muscles—it's the most
important thing. A cow weighs between eleven and seventeen hundred pounds, a horse between fifteen hundred
pounds and a ton. That's all there is to it.

Imagine a cow who's having a hard time birthing. Naturally it's night. It's really cold, the barn is dirty, and there's
barely any light.

Okay.

The cow's in pain, and the farmer's unhappy too, because that cow is his livelihood. If the vet costs him more
than the price of the meat that's about to be born, he's
gotta think twice. . . . You say:

"The calf is breeched. I just have to turn it around, and
it will come out on its own."

The cowshed comes to life. They pull their oldest kid
out of bed, and the younger one follows. For once, there's
something going on.

You get the animal tied up—nice and close. You don't
want any kicking. You strip down to a T-shirt. Now it's suddenly cold. You find a faucet and scrub your hands with
the bit of soap sitting there. You put on your gloves, which
come up to just under your armpits. Then you take your
left hand and pull on the enormous vulva, and in you go.

You go looking for the one-hundred-forty- or one-hundred-fifty-pound calf in the far reaches of the uterus, and you turn it around—with one hand.

It takes a while, but you manage. Later, back inside, you drink a little brandy to warm yourself up, and you think about your weights.

Another time, the calf won't come out. You have to open up, and that costs more. The farmer watches you, and his decision is based on the way you look. If you look confident and make a move toward your car like you're going to get your equipment, he'll say yes.

If you stand there looking at the other animals and shift your weight like you're about to leave, he'll say no.

And still another time, the calf is already dead. You have to be careful not to ruin the heifer, so you cut the calf up into little pieces and pull them out one after another, always with the glove.

When you go home later, your heart feels empty.

Years have gone by, and I'm still a long way from getting it all paid off, but everything's going well.

When old man Villemeux died, I bought his farm and fixed it up a little.

I met someone, and then he left. My big rug-beater hands, I guess.

I took in two dogs. The first one showed up on his

own and decided he liked the place. The second one had seen some rough times before I adopted him. Naturally, the second one rules the roost. There's also a handful of cats. I don't ever see them, but their bowls are always empty. And I love my garden. It's sort of a mess, but there are some old rosebushes that have been there since before my time that don't require any care from me. They're really beautiful.

A year ago I bought some teak lawn furniture. It cost a lot, but it looks like it'll hold up well.

From time to time, I go out with Marc Pardini, who teaches I don't know what at the local school. We go to the movies or out to eat. He likes to play the intellectual with me, which I find funny—because to tell the truth, I've turned into quite a hick. He loans me books and CDs.

From time to time, I sleep with him. It's always good.

Late last night, I got a phone call. It was the Billebaudes— the farm on the road to Tianville. The guy said there was some pain-in-the-ass problem and it couldn't wait.

That phone call cost me, to put it mildly. I'd had to work the weekend before, and that made thirteen days straight that I'd been working. I talked to my dogs for a while— nothing in particular, I just wanted to hear the sound of my voice—and I made myself a cup of coffee, black as ink.

The minute I pulled my key out of the ignition, I knew something was wrong. The house was dark and the cow-shed silent.

I kicked up a hell of a racket, banging on the corrugated steel door as if to wake the dead, but it was too late.

He said, "My cow's ass is all better, but how's yers? You even gotta ass? 'Round here they say you ain't no woman, you gots balls. That's what they say, ya know. So we told 'em we'd see fer oursel's."

And everything he said made the other two laugh.

I stared at their fingernails, chewed down to the flesh. You think they'd have taken me on a bale of straw? No, they were too drunk to bend down without falling over. They pinned me up against an icy tank in the dairy barn. There was a length of bent pipe grinding into my back. It was pitiful to see them struggling with their flies.

The whole thing was pitiful.

They hurt me really bad. Put like that, it doesn't mean much, but I'll say it again for those who might not have got it the first time: they hurt me really bad.

Ejaculation sobered up the Billebaude boy real quick.

"Hey, uh, doctor, we was just havin' a lil fun, right? We

don't get much chance to have no fun out here, ya know, an' my brother-in-law there, it's his bach'ler party, ain't that right, Manu?"

Manu was already sleeping, and Manu's friend was starting to booze it up again.

I said, "Of course, of course." I even joked around with him for a while, until he handed me the bottle. It was plum brandy.

The alcohol had rendered them harmless, but I gave them each a dose of Ketamine. I didn't want them twitching around. Then I saw to my own comfort.

I put on my sterile gloves and washed everything thoroughly with Betadine.

Next, I pulled the skin of the scrotum tight. With my scalpel blade I made a small incision. I pulled out the testicles. I cut. I ligated the epididymis and the vessel with catgut No. 3.5. I put it back in the sac and made a continuous suture. Good, clean work.

The one who'd been on the phone had been the most brutal, since this was his home. I grafted his balls just above his Adam's apple.

It was nearly six in the morning when I stopped by my neighbor's. Madame Brudet was seventy-two years old, and had been on her feet for a good long while—all shriveled up, but brave.

"I'm afraid I'm going to have to go away for a while, Madame Brudet. I need someone to look after my dogs, and the cats too."

"Nothing serious, I hope?"

"I don't know."

"I'll be happy to keep an eye on the cats, although I still say it's not a good idea to fatten them up like that. All they have to do is hunt field mice. The dogs . . . that's a little harder because they're so big, but if it's not for too long, I'll keep them here."

"I'll write you a check for the food."

"That's fine. Just put it behind the TV. Nothing serious, I hope?"

"Tttttt tttttt," I said with a smile.

Now, I'm sitting at my kitchen table. I've made some more coffee and I'm smoking a cigarette. I'm waiting for the police car.

I only hope they don't use the siren.

Junior

His name is Alexander Devermont. He's a young man, all pink and blond.

Raised in a vacuum. One hundred percent bar soap and Colgate with fluoride, with short-sleeved gingham shirts and a dimple on his chin. Cute. Clean. A real little suckling pig.

He's almost twenty—that discouraging age where you still think anything's possible. So many prospects and so many illusions. So many hits to take, too.

But not for this rosy young man. Life has never done him any harm. No one's ever pulled his ears till it really hurt. He's a good kid.

His mom's a social climber—she farts higher than her ass. She says, "Hello, this is Elisabeth De-vermont . . . ," separating out the first syllable. As if she still hoped to fool someone. . . . Tut tut tut. . . . You can pay to have a lot of things these days, but for the particle—those two little letters that mean your ancestors were nobles—no way.

You can't buy that sort of pride anymore. It's like Obélix, who fell into a pot of magic potion when he was a baby and ended up invincible: you have to luck into it when you're little. That doesn't stop Junior's mom from wearing a signet ring engraved with a coat of arms.

What coat of arms? I wonder. A crown and some fleurs-de-lis jumbled together on a heraldic shield. The Association of Pork Butchers and Delicatessens of France uses the same one on its syndicate letterhead, but she doesn't know that. Phew.

His dad took over the family business—a company that makes white resin lawn furniture, known as Rofitex.

Guaranteed ten years against yellowing in any climate.

Of course, resin kind of makes you think of camping trips and backyard picnics. It would've been more chic to make stuff out of teak—classy benches that would pick up a nice sheen over time, and some lichens, under the hundred-year oak that great-grandpa planted in the middle of the grounds. . . . But, oh well—you have to take what they leave you, huh?

Speaking of furniture, I was exaggerating a little when I said earlier that life had never dealt Junior any harsh blows. Of course it had. One day, while he was dancing with a young lady from a good family, flat and pedigreed like a true English setter, he had his share of angst.

It was during one of those elegant little get-togethers that the moms organize at exorbitant cost to keep their progeny from venturing one day between the breasts of some Leïla or Hannah or some other girl who reeks of heresy or Tunisian spices.

So there he was, with his neck bent and his hands sweaty. He was dancing with this girl, being extra careful not to let his fly brush against her belly. He was trying to sway his hips a little and beating the time with the heels of his Westons. Like that, you know, kind of laid-back. The way young people do.

And then the babe asked:

"So what does your father do?" (It's a question that girls ask at this sort of affair.)

He pretended to be distracted, spinning her around as he answered:

"He's the CEO at Rofitex—I dunno if you've heard of it. . . . Two hundred empl—"

She didn't give him time to finish. She stopped dancing at once and opened her setter's eyes wide:

"Hold on . . . Rofitex? . . . You mean the . . . the . . . the condoms, Rofitex?"

Now that, that was the best.

"No, the lawn furniture," he answered, but really, he'd been ready for anything but that. But really, what an airhead this girl was. What an airhead. Fortunately, the music had stopped and he could head for the buffet to drink a little champagne and digest it all. Really.

Turns out she wasn't even one of the society girls—she'd snuck in.

Twenty years old. My God.

It took young Devermont two tries to pass his graduation exam, but not the driver's test. That was all right. He just passed it, and on the first try.

Not like his brother, who had to retake it three times.

At dinner, everyone is in a good mood. It wasn't in the bag, because the local examiner is a real asshole. A drunk, too. It's the country here.

Like his brother and his cousins before him, Alexander got his license over summer vacation, out at his grandmother's place, because the fees in the provinces are a lot less than in Paris: nearly a hundred and fifty euros difference for the driver's ed course.

But finally, the drunk was more or less sober and put his scrawl on the pink slip without being a smart ass about it.

Alexander's allowed to use his mother's Golf as long as she doesn't need it. Otherwise, he's supposed to take the old Peugeot that's in the barn. Same as all the kids.

It's still in good condition, but it smells like chicken shit.

It's the end of vacation. Soon he'll have to go back to the big apartment on Avenue Mozart and get into the private business school on Avenue de Saxe. A school that's not yet accredited, but whose name is complicated, with lots of initials: the IHERP or the IRPHE or the IHEMA or something like that. (The Institute of Higher Education My Ass.)

Our little suckling pig has changed a lot over the summer. He's been dissolute—he's even started smoking.

Marlboro Lights.

It's because of the new company he's keeping: he's gotten chummy with the son of a big local farmer, Franck Mingeaut. This kid is a piece of work—filthy rich, flashy, rowdy, and loud. Says "hello" politely to Alexander's grand-mother and checks out his younger cousins at the same time. Tsk-tsk.

Franck Mingeaut is happy to know Junior. Thanks to him, he can enter society, go to parties where the girls are slen-der and pretty and where they serve the families' own champagne instead of cheap Valstar beer. Instinct tells him that this is the way to go if he wants to land himself a nice cushy setup. The back rooms of cafés, unsophisticated Marylines, pool tables, county fairs—none of that stuff lasts. Whereas an evening with the Widget girl in her home at Chateau Widgetière . . . now there's energy well spent.

Junior Devermont is happy with his *nouveau riche* friend. Thanks to him, he skids through gravel courtyards in his sports convertible, he charges down the back roads of the Touraine, giving rednecks the finger to get them to move their Renaults out of his way, and he treats his father like crap. He leaves an extra shirt button open, and he's even started wearing the pendant from his baptism again, like a tough guy still tender at heart. The girls eat it up.

Tonight is *the* party of the summer. The count and countess of La Rochepoucaut are receiving in honor of their youngest daughter, Éléonore. All the upper crust will be there—from Mayenne down to the far end of Berry, from the Society Pages, you name it. Young virgin heiresses as if they grew on trees.

Money. Not the flashiness of money; the odor of it. Low necklines, creamy complexions, pearl necklaces, ultra-light cigarettes, and nervous laughter. For Franck-of-the-bracelet and Alexander-of-the-fine-chain, this is the big night.

No way they're going to miss this.

To those people, a rich farmer will always be a peasant, and a well-brought-up industrialist will always be a tradesman. All the more reason to drink their champagne and jump their daughters in the bushes. The young ladies aren't all antisocial. They're direct descendents of the crusader Godefroy de Bouillon, and they have no problem pushing the last crusade a little further.

Franck doesn't have an invitation, but Junior knows the guy at the door—no problem, you slip him twenty euros and he'll let you in. He'll even bark out your name like they do at the Automobile Club shows if you want.

The big hitch is the car. The car makes all the difference if you want to cinch the deal with the ones who don't like prickly bushes.

If some pretty young thing doesn't want to leave too early, she'll bid her daddy good night and find an escort to take her home. If you haven't got a car out here, where everyone lives miles apart, you're either hopeless or a virgin.

And right now the situation is critical. Franck doesn't have his chick magnet—it's in for service—and Alexander doesn't have his mother's car. She took it back to Paris.

What else is there? The sky-blue Peugeot with the chicken droppings on the seats and along the doors. There's even straw on the floor and a "Hunting Is Natural" bumper sticker on the back. God, it's disgusting.

"What about your father? Where's he?"

"Out of town."

"And his car?"

"Uh . . . it's here. Why?"

"Why's it here?"

"Because Jean-Raymond has to detail it."

(Jean-Raymond's the groundskeeper.)

"That's brilliant! We'll borrow his car for the night and bring it right back. There you go—what he doesn't know won't hurt him."

"Uh-uh, Franck, that's not an option. Not an option."

"Why not?"

"Listen, if anything should happen, I'm dead. Uh-uh, it's not an option. . . ."

"But what do you think's gonna happen, ass-wipe? Huh? Just what do you think's gonna happen?"

"Uh-uh . . ."

"Holy shit! Knock it off with that 'uh-uh'—what the hell does that mean? It's fifteen kilometers there and fifteen back. The road is perfectly straight and there won't be a soul out at that hour, so just tell me, what's the problem?"

"If we should get into any shit at all . . ."

"*But what* kind of shit? Huh? *What* kind of shit? I've had my license for three years and I've never had one single problem, do you hear me? Not one."

He flicks his front tooth with his thumb as if to yank it loose.

"Uh-uh—no way. Not my dad's Jag."

"Fuck, this can't be for real, are you really this stupid? This can't be for real!"

". . ."

"So what are we gonna do then? We show up at La Roche-my-balls in your shitty henhouse on wheels?"

"Well, yeah. . . ."

"Hold on—weren't we supposed to pick up your cousin and her girlfriend at Saint-Chinan?"

"Well, yeah. . . ."

"And you think they're gonna put their pretty little asses on your shit-covered seats?!"

"Well, no. . . ."

"Well, what, then? . . . We borrow your dad's wheels, we ride in style, and in a few hours we put it ever-so-gently back where it came from. And that's that."

"Uh-uh, not the Jag . . ." (silence) ". . . not the Jag."

"Listen, I'm gonna find someone else to take me. You're such a stupid shit—it's the party of the summer, and you want us to show up in your cattle truck. Out of the question. Does it even run?"

"Yeah, it runs."

"Fuuuck, this can't be for real. . . ."

He pulls on the skin of his cheeks.

"Anyway, without me, you can't get in."

"Yeah, well, between not going at all or going in your piece of shit, I don't know which is worse. . . . Hey, watch out there aren't still chickens in it!"

On the road home. Five in the morning. Two drunk, tired boys who smell like cigarettes and sweat but not fornication. (Nice party, luck of the draw . . . it happens.)

Two silent boys on the D49 between Bonneuil and Cissé-le-Duc in Indre-et-Loire.

"Well, see . . . We didn't crash it. . . . Hey, you see . . . It wasn't worth pissing me off with all your uh-uhs. Big ol' Jean-Raymond can polish your daddy's car tomorrow. . . ."

"Pfff. . . . Lot of good it did us. . . . We might as well have taken the other one. . . ."

"You got that right. Suck it up. . . ."

He touches his crotch.

". . . Not a lot of action for you, huh? . . . Anyway . . .
I'm hooking up with a blonde with big tits tomorrow, to
play tennis. . . ."

"Which one?"

"You know, the one that—"

He never finished his sentence because a wild boar, a pig of
at least three hundred pounds, crossed the road just at that
moment, but without looking either right or left, the brute.

A wild boar in a great big hurry who was maybe on his
way home from a party and afraid his parents were going
to yell.

First they heard the screeching of tires, and then an
enormous *thunk* up front. Alexander Devermont said:

"Well, shit."

They stopped the car. They left their doors open and
went to check it out—the stiff, dead pig and the stiff, dead
front end of the car: no more fender, no more radiator, no
more headlights, and no more body. Even the little Jaguar
hood ornament had taken a hit. Alexander Devermont
said again:

"Well, shit."

He was too tipsy and too tired to say anything more.
Still, at that precise moment, he was already clearly con-

scious of the immense expanse of shit that was waiting for him. He was *clearly* conscious of it.

Franck gave the boar a kick in the paunch and said:

"Well, we're not leaving it here. At least if we bring it back, we can have a barbeque. . . ."

Alexander started to laugh very quietly:

"Yeah, that's good stuff, roast boar. . . ."

It wasn't at all funny—actually, the situation was somewhat tragic—but they got the giggles. Doubtless because they were so tired and nervous.

"Your mom's gonna be so happy. . . ."

"Oh, yeah—she's gonna be thrilled!"

And those two little jackasses laughed so hard their stomachs hurt.

"Okay, then. . . . Shove it in the trunk? . . ."

"Yeah."

"Shit!"

"What now?!"

"It's full of crap. . . ."

"Huh?"

"I'm telling you, it's full! . . . Your dad's got his golf bag in there, and cases of wine. . . ."

"Shit. . . ."

"What do we do?"

"We'll put it in the back, on the floor. . . ."

"You think?"

"Yeah, hold on. I'll put something down to protect the seats. . . . Look in the back of the trunk—see if you can't find a duvet. . . ."

"A what?"

"A duvet."

"What's that?"

". . . That thing with the green and blue squares, all the way in the back. . . ."

"Oh, the comforter! . . . A fancy-schmancy Parisian one. . . ."

"Yeah, whatever. . . . Come on, hurry up."

"Hold on, I'll help you. No point staining his leather seats, too. . . ."

"Got that right."

"Fuck, he's heavy! . . . "

"No shit."

"He stinks, too."

"Hey, Alex . . . it's the country. . . ."

"Screw the country."

They got back in the car. No problem getting it started again—at least nothing happened to the motor. That's something, anyway.

And then a few miles farther on: a big, big fright. It started with some noises and groans behind them.

Franck said:

"Fuck—he's not dead, the bastard!"

Alexander didn't answer. Enough was enough, already.

The pig started to get back up and turn every which way.

Franck slammed on the brakes and yelled:

"Let's get out of here!"

He was all white.

They slammed the doors shut and moved away from the car. Inside, it was total shit.

Total Shit.

The cream-colored leather seats, destroyed. The steering wheel, destroyed. The elm-veneered gearshift, destroyed; the headrests, destroyed. The whole interior of the car, destroyed, destroyed, destroyed.

Devermont Junior, devastated.

The animal's eyes were popping out of their sockets, and there was a white foam around his big curving teeth. It was a horrible sight.

They decided to hide behind the door, pull it open, and then climb up and take refuge on the roof. It might have been a good plan, but they never would find out, be-

cause in the meantime the pig had stomped on the auto-
matic lock and locked himself inside.

And the key was still in the dash.

Oh, that . . . you could say, when it all goes to hell, it all
goes to hell.

Franck Mingeaut pulled his cell phone out from the pocket
of his chic dinner jacket and dialed 911, totally embarrassed.

When the firemen arrived, the beast had calmed down
a little. Barely. Let's just say there was nothing left to destroy.

The fire chief walked around the car. Really, he was
impressed. He couldn't help saying:

"Such a beautiful car—that's gotta hurt."

This next part is unbearable for those people who like
nice things. . . .

One of the men went to get an enormous shotgun, a
sort of bazooka. He moved away from the rest of the
group and took aim. The pig and the window exploded
at the same time.

The interior of the car was freshly painted: red.

Blood everywhere—even at the back of the glove com-
partment, even between the numbers on the in-dash phone.

Alexander Devermont was in a daze. You'd have thought
he wasn't thinking anymore. At all. About anything. Or

only about burying himself alive or turning the fireman's bazooka on himself.

But no, he was thinking about the local gossips and about what a windfall this was going to be for the ecologists. . . .

It must be said that not only did his father have a magnificent Jaguar, but he'd also set his tenacious political sights on fighting the Greens.

The Greens wanted to outlaw hunting and create a Nature Park and whatever else besides, just when it would be a pain in the ass for the big landowners.

It was a battle that he enjoyed enormously and that he'd nearly won up to this point. Just last night at the dinner table, while he was carving the duck, he'd said:

"Look! Here's one that Grolet and his bunch of ass-combers won't be seeing in their binoculars anymore! Ha, ha, ha!"

But this . . . the wild boar exploding into a thousand pieces in the future regional councillor's Jaguar Sovereign—that's got to chafe a little. Surely a little, doesn't it?

There's even fur stuck to the windows.

The firemen leave; the cops leave. Tomorrow a tow truck will come take care of the . . . that . . . well . . . the metallic gray thing blocking the road.

Our two friends walk down the road, dinner jackets tossed over their shoulders. There's nothing to say. Anyway, at the point things are at, it's not even worth thinking about it anymore, either.

Franck says:

"You want a cigarette?"

Junior answers:

"Yeah, I'd really like one."

They walk like that for a while. The sun is coming up over the fields. The sky is pink and some stars are still lingering. There's not the slightest noise—only the rustling of rabbits running through the grass in the ditch.

And then Alexander Devermont turns to his friend and says:

"So? . . . This blonde, now, that you were telling me about . . . the one with the big tits. . . . Who is this girl?"

And his friend smiles at him.

For Years

For years I believed that this woman was outside my life—not very far maybe, but *outside.*

That she didn't exist anymore, that she lived far away, that she had never been all that beautiful, that she belonged to the world of the past. The world back when I was young and romantic, when I believed that love lasted forever and that there wasn't anything greater than my love for her. All that foolishness.

I was twenty-six years old, and I was on the platform at a train station. I couldn't understand why she was crying so much, and held her in my arms and buried my face in her neck. I thought she was sad because I was leaving, and she was letting me see her distress. And then a few weeks later, after I'd walked all over my pride like a fool on the phone and whined on and on in letters that were too long, I finally understood.

That she'd broken down that last day because she knew she was looking at my face for the last time. That she was crying over me—over my mortal remains. And that she wasn't happy to see me that way.

For months, I bumped up against everything.

I couldn't focus on anything and I bumped up against everything. The worse I felt, the more I bumped up against things.

I was an absolute wreck, but I pulled it off pretty well. Day after empty day, I managed to put a good face on. I'd get up, work 'til I was ready to drop, eat like I was supposed to, drink beer with the guys I worked with, and have a good laugh with my brothers. But that whole time, if any of them had so much as flicked his finger against my skin, it would've broken me clean in half.

But I'm not being entirely honest with myself. It wasn't courage. It was stupidity—because I thought she'd come back. I really believed she would.

I hadn't seen anything coming, and my heart had completely come apart on a train platform one Sunday night. I couldn't come to terms with it, and I kept bumping up against anything and everything.

The years that followed had no effect on me. Some days I'd be surprised to think:

"You know? . . . That's strange . . . I don't think I thought about her yesterday. . . ." But instead of congratulating myself, I'd wonder how that could've happened—how I'd managed to go a whole day without thinking of her. I was especially obsessed with her name. That and two or three very precise images of her—always the same ones.

It's true. Every morning I put my feet on the ground, ate, showered, got dressed, and went to work.

Every now and then I'd see a girl naked. Every now and then, but without any tenderness.

Emotions: nil.

And then at last, in spite of all that, I got another chance—although by then I really didn't care anymore.

Another woman met me. A very different woman, with a different name. She fell in love with me and decided to make me a whole man. Without asking my opinion, she set me back on my feet and married me, less than a year after our first kiss, exchanged in an elevator during a conference.

An unhoped-for woman. I have to admit: I was petrified. I didn't believe in any of it anymore, and I must have frequently hurt her. I'd caress her belly, and my mind would wander. I'd lift her hair and hope to find another scent there. She never said a word. She knew my phantom life wouldn't last long. Not when I had her laughter, not when I had her skin, not when I had this whole jumble of basic, unconditional love that she was ready to give me. She was right: My phantom life let me live in peace.

She's in the next room right now. She is sleeping.

On a professional level, I never could have guessed I'd be this successful. Maybe it pays to be hard, maybe I was in the right place at the right time, maybe I made some good decisions . . . I don't know.

At any rate, I see clearly in the eyes of my old class-mates, as much surprised as suspicious, that it all discon-certs them: the pretty wife, the fancy business card, the shirts tailor-made to fit . . . especially since I started out with so little. It's perplexing.

Back then, above all, I was the guy who thought of nothing but girls . . . well, of nothing but *this* girl. I was the guy who wrote letters every day during lectures and who didn't look at the asses or breasts or eyes or anything else on the café terraces. The guy who took the first train to Paris every Friday and who came back sad on Monday mornings, with circles under his eyes, cursing the distance and the conductor's zeal. More harlequin than golden boy, it's true.

Since I loved her, I neglected my studies. And since I was blowing off my studies, and vacillating on other things, she dumped me. She must've thought the future was too . . . uncertain with a guy like me.

When I read my bank statements today, I see very well that life is quite a jokester.

So I went on with my life as if nothing had happened.

Of course, just for fun, every now and then my wife and I would talk about our student days, either on our own or with friends. We'd talk about the movies and books that had shaped us, and *the loves of our youth*—faces we'd forgotten over time, which some little coincidence happened to make us think of. The price of a cup of coffee and all that sort of nostalgia. . . . It was like that part of our lives was sitting on a shelf. We'd dust it off from time to time, but I never dwelled on it. Oh, no.

For a while, I remember, every day I passed a sign that had the name of the town where I knew she lived, with the number of kilometers.

Every morning on my way to my office and every night on the way back, I'd glance at the sign. I glanced at it—that's all. I never followed it. I thought about it, but even the idea of flipping on my turn signal seemed like spitting on my wife.

Still, I did glance at it, it's true.

And then I changed jobs. No more sign.

But there were always other reasons, other pretexts. Always. How many times did I turn around on the street, my heart in a tailspin because I thought I'd caught sight of a silhouette that . . . or a voice that . . . or a head of hair like . . . ?

How many times?

I thought I didn't think about her anymore, but all it took was to be alone for just one minute in a more or less quiet place, and she'd come back to me.

On the terrace of a restaurant one day—it was less than six months ago—when the client I'd invited didn't show up, I went looking for her in my memories. I loosened my collar and sent the waiter to buy me a pack of cigarettes—the strong, acrid ones I used to smoke way back when. I stretched out my legs and refused to let the waiter clear off the place setting across from me. I ordered a good wine, a Gruaud-Larose, I think . . . and as I smoked, eyes half closed, savoring a little ray of sun, I watched her coming toward me.

I watched and watched. I couldn't stop thinking about her—and about what we'd done when we were together and slept in the same bed.

I never once asked myself whether I still loved her or what my exact feelings toward her were. That would serve no purpose. But I loved to find her at the detour of a moment of solitude. I must say it, because it's the truth.

Fortunately for me, my life didn't leave me many moments of solitude. Honestly, the only time it ever happened was if some client forgot me completely or if I was alone in my car at night, with nothing else to worry about. In other words, almost never.

And even if I wanted to let myself indulge in a good dose of blues, of nostalgia—to assume a joking tone, for example, and try to find her phone number on the Internet or some other nonsense of the sort—I know now that it's out of the question, because for the past several years I've had some real safeguards. The fiercest kind: my kids.

I'm crazy about my kids. I've got three: a big girl, Marie, who's seven; another who'll soon be four, Joséphine; and Yvan, the baby of the family, who's not quite two. Besides, I'm the one who begged my wife to give me a third. I remember her talking about fatigue and the future . . . but I love babies so much, their gibberish and their wet kisses. "Go ahead," I told her, "make me another baby." She didn't hold out for long—and for that alone, I know that she's my only friend and that I'll never leave her. Even if I do brush shoulders with a tenacious shadow.

My kids are the best thing that ever happened to me.

An old love story doesn't count for anything next to that. Nothing at all.

So that's more or less how I've lived . . . and then last week, she said her name on the phone:

"It's Hélèna."

"Hélèna?"

"I'm not interrupting?"

My little boy was on my knees, trying to grab the phone and squealing.

"Well . . ."

"Is that your kid?"

"Yes."

"How old is he?"

". . . Why are you calling me like this?"

"How old is he?"

"Twenty months."

"I'm calling because I'd like to see you."

"You want to see me?"

"Yes."

"What is this shit?"

". . ."

"Just like that. You said to yourself, 'Hey! . . . I think I'd like to see him again. . . .'"

"Almost like that."

"Why? . . . I mean, why now? . . . After all these ye—"

"Twelve years. It's been twelve years."

"Okay. So? . . . What happened? It just hit you? What do you want? You want to know how old my kids are or if I've lost my hair or . . . or see what effect you'd have on me or . . . or just like that, to talk about the good old days?!"

"Listen, I didn't think you'd take it like this—I'm going to let you go. I'm sorry. I . . ."

"How did you get my number?"

"From your father."

"What!"

"I called your father earlier and asked him for your number, that's all."

"Did he remember you?"

"No. Well . . . I didn't tell him who I was."

I put my son down and he went to join his sisters in their bedroom. My wife wasn't home.

"Hold on, don't hang up. . . . Marie! Can you put his booties back on, please? . . . Hello? Are you there?"

"Yes."

"Well? . . ."

"Well, what? . . ."

"You want to get together sometime?"

"Yes. Well, not for long. Just to have a drink or walk around for a little while, you know. . . ."

"Why? What for?"

"I just want to see you again—to talk to you for a little while."

"Hélèna?"

"Yes."

"Why are you doing this?"

"Why?"

"Yes, why are you calling me? Why so late? Why now? You didn't even ask yourself whether you might be throwing shit into my life. . . . You just dial my number and you—"

"Listen, Pierre. I'm going to die."

". . ."

"I'm calling you now because I'm going to die. I don't know when exactly, but before very long."

I pulled the phone away from my face as though to get a little air. I tried to stand up, but without success.

"That can't be true."

"Yes, it's true."

"What's the matter?"

"Oh . . . it's complicated. To make a long story short, you could say that my blood is . . . Well, I don't even know anymore just what it is now because the diagnoses are confusing. But in the end, it's pretty serious."

I said:

"You're sure?"

"What? What do you think? You think I'd make up some over-the-top sob story just to have a reason to call you?!"

"I'm sorry."

"Okay."

"Maybe they made a mistake."

"Yes . . . maybe."

"You don't think so?"

"No. I don't think so."

"How is this possible?"

"I don't know."

"Are you in pain?"

"Not really."

"Are you in pain?"

"Well, a little."

"And you want to see me again *one last time*?"

"Yes. You could put it that way."

". . ."

". . ."

"You're not worried that I'll disappoint you? You wouldn't rather hold on to a . . . good impression?"

"An impression from when you were young and handsome?"

I could hear her smile.

"Exactly. When I was young and handsome and didn't have gray hair yet. . . ."

"You have gray hair?!"

"I've got five, I think."

"Ah! Okay, then—you had me worried! You're right. I don't know if it's a good idea, but I've been thinking about it for a while . . . and I told myself that it was one thing that would really make me happy. . . . So since there aren't many things that make me happy anymore . . . I . . . I called you."

"How long have you been thinking about this?"

"For twelve years! No . . . I'm kidding. I've been thinking about it for several months. Since my last stay in the hospital, to be exact."

"You really want to see me again, you think?"

"Yes."

"When?"

"Whenever you want. Whenever you can."

"Where do you live?"

"Same place. A hundred kilometers from you, I think."

"Hélèna?"

"Yes."

"No, never mind."

"You're right. Never mind. That's how it is, that's life. I'm not calling you to unravel the past or to build castles in the sky, you know. I . . .

"I'm calling you because I want to see your face again. That's all. It's like when people go back to the village where they spent their childhood or to their parents' house . . . or to whatever place touched their life."

"Like some kind of pilgrimage."

I realized that my voice sounded different.

"Yes, exactly—it's like a pilgrimage. I guess your face is a place that touched my life."

"Pilgrimages are always so sad."

"Why do you say that?! Have you ever made one!?"

"No. Yes. To Lourdes. . . ."

"Oh, well, okay, then . . . okay, then, Lourdes, of course. . . ."

She forced herself to use a mocking tone.

I could hear the kids squabbling, and I didn't feel like talking anymore. I wanted to hang up. I ended up saying:

"When?"

"You tell me."

"Tomorrow?"

"If you like."

"Where?" .

"Halfway between our two towns—in Sully, for example. . . ."

"Are you able to drive?"

"Yes. I can drive."

"What's in Sully?"

"Well, not much, I would guess. . . . We'll see. We can just meet in front of the town hall. . . ."

"At lunchtime?"

"Oh, no. I'm not much fun to eat with, you know. . . ."

She forced out another laugh.

". . . After lunch would be better."

He couldn't fall asleep that night. He stared at the ceiling, eyes open wide. He wanted to keep them good and dry. Not to cry.

It wasn't because of his wife. He was afraid of deceiving himself, of making a mistake—of crying more because of the death of his inner life than because of her death. He knew that if he got started, he wouldn't be able to stop.

Mustn't open the floodgates. Absolutely not. Because for so many years now he'd been a show-off, grumbling about people's weaknesses. Other people's. People who didn't know what they wanted, who dragged all their mediocrity along behind them.

For so many years he'd looked back on his youth with such fucking tenderness. Whenever he thought of her, he always got philosophical. He always pretended to smile over it or to understand something from it—whereas in reality he'd never understood a thing.

He knows perfectly well that he's never loved anyone but her and that he's never been loved by anyone but her. That she was his only love and that nothing will ever be able to change that. That she dropped him like a cumbersome, useless thing. That she never reached out a hand to him, never dropped him a line to encourage him to get back on his feet—to confess that she wasn't really doing all that great. That he was wrong. That he deserved better than her. Or even that she'd made the mistake of her life and that she'd regretted it in secret. He knew how proud she was—to tell him that for twelve years she'd been suffering, too, and that now she was going to die. . . .

He didn't want to cry. He told himself all sorts of things to keep the tears back—all sorts of things. Then his wife rolled over, putting her hand on his stomach, and immediately he regretted his delusions. Of course he'd loved and been loved by another—of course. He looks at this face next to him, and he takes her hand and kisses it. She smiles in her sleep.

No, he has nothing to complain about. He has no reason to lie to himself. Romantic passion, hey, ho, that only lasts a moment. And now enough of that, huh? Plus, tomorrow afternoon doesn't work out too well, because he's got an appointment with the guys from Sygma II. He's going to have to put Marcheron in charge, and that's another problem altogether, because with Marcheron. . . .

He hadn't been able to fall asleep that night. He thought about all sorts of things.

That's how he'd explain his insomnia. But his lamp doesn't cast much light, and he can't see a thing. And, just like back in the days of his great sorrows, he bumps up against everything.

She couldn't fall asleep that night, either, but she's used to it. She almost never sleeps anymore. It's because she doesn't tire herself out enough during the day—that's the doctor's theory. Her sons are at their father's, and all she does is cry.

Cry. Cry. Cry.

She's breaking up—dropping the ballast and letting herself go under. She doesn't care. She thinks that everything's fine now. It's time to move on to something else and clear the stage. It's all very well for the doctor to say she's not tiring herself out—he doesn't know a thing about it, with his neat white coat and his complicated words. To tell the truth, she's exhausted. Exhausted.

She cries because, finally, she called Pierre. She always managed to keep track of his phone number, and several times she went so far as to dial the ten numbers that separated her from him. She'd hear his voice and hang up right away. One time, she even followed him for a whole day. She wanted to know where he lived, what kind of car he drove, where he worked, how he dressed, and whether he seemed worried. She followed his wife, too. She'd had to admit that his wife was cheerful and pretty, and that she'd had kids with him.

She cries because her heart started beating again today, and for some time now she hadn't thought that was possible anymore. She's had a harder life than she'd have imagined. She's mostly known solitude. She thought it was too late now to feel anything—that her good days were over. Especially since *they* got all worked up one day over a blood test, a routine exam that she happened to have done because she felt a little out of sorts. Everyone, from the little doctors to the great professors, had an opinion about her condition— but not much to say when it came to getting rid of it.

She cries for so many reasons that she doesn't want to think about it. Her whole life comes flying back in her face. So, to protect herself a little, she tells herself that she's crying for the sake of crying and that's all there is to it.

She was already there when I arrived. She smiled and said, "This must be the first time I didn't keep you waiting! See—there was no need to lose hope." I told her I hadn't lost hope.

We didn't hug. I said, "You haven't changed." It's a dumb thing to say, but it's what I thought, except that I thought she was more beautiful than ever. She was very pale, and you could see all the little blue veins around her eyes, on her eyelids, and at her temples. She'd gotten thin, and the hollows in her face were deeper than before. She seemed more resigned, whereas I remember the air of vivacity she used to exude. She never stopped looking at me. She wanted me to talk to her; she wanted me to be quiet. She smiled the whole time. She'd wanted to see me again. For my part, I didn't know how to move my hands, or if I could smoke or touch her arm.

It was a creepy town. We walked as far as the public garden a little farther on.

We told each other the stories of our lives. It was somewhat disjointed. We each kept our secrets. She had trouble finding the right words. At one point, she asked me the difference between helplessness and idleness. I couldn't remember. She made a gesture to show that, anyhow, it didn't really matter. She said that it had all made her too bitter, or too hard—in any case, too different from what she'd been before.

We barely touched on the subject of her illness, except when she talked about her kids: she said it was no life for them. Not long ago, she'd wanted to cook them some noodles, but she hadn't even been able to manage that, because the pot of water was too heavy for her to lift. And really, that was no life. They'd had more than their share of sadness up to now.

She made me talk about my wife and kids and work. And even about Marcheron. She wanted to know everything, but I could tell that most of the time she wasn't listening.

We were sitting on a peeling bench, across from a fountain that must not have spit any water since the day of its inauguration. Everything was ugly. Sad and ugly. A light mist was beginning to fall, and we sort of shrunk into ourselves to keep warm.

Finally, she got up. It was time for her to go.

She said, "I have just one favor I'd like to ask, just one. I want to smell you." And when I didn't respond, she confessed that through all these years she'd wanted to breathe in my scent. I kept my hands all the way in the bottoms of my coat pockets, because otherwise . . .

She went behind me and leaned over my hair. She stayed like that for a long time, and I felt terrible. Next, she moved her nose to the hollow at the nape of my neck and all around my head, taking her time, and then she went down the length of my neck to my collar. She breathed in. She kept her hands behind her back, too. Next, she loosened my tie and opened the first two buttons of my shirt. I felt the tip of her nostrils all cold against the base of my collarbone, and I . . . I . . .

I shifted somewhat abruptly. She stood back up behind me and put both hands flat on my shoulders. She said, "I'm going to go. I want you not to move and not to turn around. Please—I'm begging you. I'm begging you."

I didn't move. I didn't want to, anyway, because I didn't want her to see me with my eyes swollen and my face all contorted.

I waited a while, then headed to my car.

Clic-Clac

For five and a half months now I've wanted Sarah Briot, director of sales.

Would it not be better for me to say: for five and a half months now I've been *in love* with Sarah Briot, director of sales? I don't know.

During all this time, I haven't been able to think of her without getting a massive erection, and since it's the first time this has happened to me, I'm not sure what to call it, this sentiment.

Sarah Briot knows something's up. No, she hasn't ever bumped up against my pants or anything, but she knows.

Of course, she doesn't realize that it'll be five and a half months on Tuesday, because she doesn't pay as much attention to numbers as I do. (I'm an account auditor, so it's only natural. . . .) But I know she knows, because she's sharp.

She speaks to men in a way that shocked me before and that now drives me to despair. She speaks to them as if she's got special glasses, the Superman X-ray kind, that let her see the exact size of the sex of whatever guy she's talking to.

The size at rest, I mean. So, obviously, that makes for some entertaining interactions at work. . . . You can imagine.

She'll shake your hand, answer your questions, smile at you, even have coffee with you in the cafeteria, from a plastic cup . . . and you, like a dumbass, all you can think about is pressing your knees together or crossing your legs. It's sheer hell.

The worst of it is that the whole time, she never stops looking you in the eye—and only in the eye.

Sarah Briot isn't beautiful. She's cute, and that's not the same thing.

She's not very tall. She's blond, but it doesn't take a genius to see that it's not her real color—those are highlights.

Like most girls, she wears pants often, and even more often, jeans. Which is too bad.

Sarah Briot is just a tiny little hair overweight. I often

hear her discussing different diets on the phone with her girlfriends. (Since she talks loud and I'm in the office next door, I hear everything.)

She says she's got to lose 9 pounds to get down to 110. I think about that every day, because I jotted it down on my desk blotter while she was talking: "119!!!"

That's also how I found out that she'd already tried the Montignac Method and that she'd have been "better off keeping the fifteen euros" . . . that she'd ripped out the center section from the April issue of *Biba*, with all Estelle Hallyday's *special weight loss* recipes . . . that she had a giant poster in her tiny kitchen showing calorie counts for every food . . . and that she'd even bought a little kitchen scale to weigh everything, like they do at Weight Watchers.

She talks about it a lot with her friend Marie, who's tall and thin, from what I gather.

(Between you and me, it's stupid, because I don't see what her girlfriend could have to say to her about it. . . .)

At this point in my story, any moron's probably wondering, "So what exactly does he see in this girl?"

Hold on . . . I'll put a stop to that!

The other day I heard Sarah Briot laughing gleefully as she told someone (Marie maybe?) how she'd ended up pawning the scale off on her mother so she could make Sarah "yummy cakes on Sundays." She got a big kick out of telling that story.

Besides, Sarah Briot isn't vulgar . . . she's alluring. Everything about her inspires caresses. And that's not the same thing, either.

So shut up.

The week before Mother's Day, I was strolling through the lingerie department at the Galeries Lafayette one day during my lunch break. All the saleswomen—a red rose in the topmost buttonhole—were on full alert, on the lookout for indecisive dads.

I'd tucked my briefcase under my arm and was playing if-I-were-married-to-Sarah-Briot-what-would-I-buy-her? . . .

Lou, Passionata, Simone Pérèle, Lejaby, Aubade. . . . My head was spinning.

Some things seemed too naughty—it was Mother's Day, after all. Others, I didn't like the color or the saleswoman. (I like foundation just fine, but still, there are limits.)

Not to mention all the styles I didn't understand.

I had a hard time seeing myself unfastening all those tiny little microscopic buttons in the heat of the action, and I couldn't figure out how the garter belt worked. (To do it right, do you leave the garters on or take them off?)

I felt hot.

I finally found, for the future mother of my children, a Christian Dior bra-and-panty set in a very pale gray silk. Classy.

"What size bra does madaaame wear?"

I set my briefcase down between my feet.

"About like this . . . ," I said, curving my hands about six inches in front of my chest.

"You have no idea?" asked the saleswoman, a little dryly. "What are her measurements?"

"Um, she comes up to about here on me . . . ," I answered, indicating my shoulder.

"I see. . . ." She pursed her lips in consternation. "I'll tell you what, I'll give you a 34C—it might be too big, but she can exchange it without a problem. Be sure to keep the receipt, okay?"

"Thank you. That's fine," I said, trying to sound like the kind of guy who takes his kids out to the woods every Sunday, without forgetting the canteens and rain jackets.

"And for the panties? Do you want the classic style or the tanga? I also have it in a G-string, but I don't think that's what you're looking for. . . ."

What do you know about it, Madame Micheline of the Galeries Lafayette?

Obviously you don't know *the* Sarah Briot of Chopard &

Minont's. The one who always lets the tip of her belly button show and who walks into other people's offices without knocking.

But when she showed it to me, I lost my nerve. No, it couldn't really be possible that someone could wear a thing like that. Seriously, it was practically an instrument of torture. I got the tanga, which ". . . has all the Brazilian touches but is less scooped over the hips this year, as you can see for yourself. Shall I gift wrap it for you, monsieur?"

A tanga.

Whew.

I shoved the little pink package between my Paris map and a couple of files, and I went back to my computer screen.

Talk about a lunch break.

At least when there are kids, it'll be easier to pick things out. I'll have to tell them: "No, kids, not a waffle iron. . . . Let's see. . . ."

It was Sittier, my colleague from exports, who said to me one day:

"You like her, huh?"

We were at Mario's splitting the lunch bill, and this

jerk wanted to act like we were old pals and go ahead, tell me everything so I can cuff you in the ribs.

"No shit. . . . You've got good taste, huh!"

I didn't feel like talking to him—not in the least.

"I guess she's quite a sexpot, huh. . . ." (Big wink.)

I shook my head disapprovingly.

"Dujoignot told me . . ."

"Dujoignot went out with her!"

I was lost in my accounts.

"Nah, but he heard a thing or two from Movard, because Movard had her, and from what I hear . . ."

He sat there, jerking his hand in the air like he was trying to shake it dry, making the little O of mOron with his mouth.

". . . Yeah, that Briot's hot, all right. . . . Not exactly inhibited, huh. . . . She'll do shit, I can't even begin to tell you. . . ."

"So don't. Who's this Movard?"

"He used to be in advertising, but he left before you got here. Our little pond was too small for him, you know how it goes. . . ."

"I see."

Poor Sittier. He doesn't finish his thought. He must be picturing a whole slew of sexual positions.

Poor Sittier. You know, my sisters call you Shittier, and

they still giggle whenever they think about your Ford Pinto.

Poor Sittier, who tried to come on to Myriam even though he wears a gold signet ring engraved with his initials.

Poor Sittier. Who still thinks he's got a chance with smart girls, and who goes on first dates with his cell phone in a plastic cover attached to his belt, and his car radio under his arm.

Poor Sittier. If you only knew how my sisters talk about you . . . when they talk about you at all.

You never know what's going to happen—how things are going to unfold, or when the simplest things are suddenly going to take on demented proportions. Take me, for example. My whole life turned upside down because of five ounces of gray silk.

For five years and not quite eight months I've lived with my sisters in a twelve-hundred-square-foot apartment near the Convention metro station.

In the beginning, it was just me and my sister Fanny. She's four years younger than I and a med student at René Descartes University. It was our parents' idea, to be economical and to make sure the little one wouldn't get lost in Paris. She'd never known anything but our hometown, Tulle, its high school, its cafés, its rebuilt mopeds.

I get on well with Fanny: She doesn't talk much, and she's always okay with anything.

For example, if it's her week to do the cooking and I bring home, say, sole, because that's what I happen to be in the mood for, she's not the kind of person to whine that I'm upsetting all her plans. She adapts.

It's not exactly the same with Myriam.

Myriam is the oldest. We're not even a year apart, but if you saw us, you wouldn't even imagine that we were brother and sister. She talks nonstop. Sometimes I think she's a little off her rocker, but that's to be expected, I guess—she's the artist in the family. . . .

After she finished her studies at the Beaux-Arts, she did photography, collages with hemp and steel wool, video clips with paint stains on the lenses, stuff with her body, creations of spaces with Loulou de La Rochette (?), demos, sculpture, dance, and I forget what else.

These days she's painting stuff I have trouble understanding, no matter how much I scrunch up my eyes. Myriam says that on the day they handed out artistic ability, I stayed home. She says I don't know how to see what's beautiful. Whatever.

The last time we got into it was when we went to the Boltanski exhibit together. (But whose idea was it to take me to see that . . . seriously. Can you imagine what a dumbass I looked like trying to figure out which way you were supposed to walk through the exhibit?)

Myriam's a real artichoke heart—she's always falling in love. Every six months since the age of fifteen (which must make it about thirty-eight times, if I'm not mistaken), she's brought us the man of her life. Mr. Good, Mr. Right, Mr. White-Wedding, Mr. Okay-This-Time-It's-For-Real, Mr. Last-One, Mr. Sure-Thing, Mr. Last-of-the-Last-Ones.

All of Europe, just for her: Yoann was Swedish; Giuseppe, Italian; Erick, Dutch; Kiko, Spanish; and Laurent, from Saint-Quentin-en-Yvelines. Obviously, there are thirty-three others. . . . At the moment, their names aren't coming back to me.

When I left my studio to move in with Fanny, Myriam was with Kiko. A brilliant future director.

At first, we didn't see much of her. Every now and then the two of them would invite themselves to dinner, and Kiko would bring the wine. It was always very good. (A good thing, since that's the only thing he had to do all day long—choose the wine.)

I liked Kiko. He'd give my sister a doleful look and then pour himself some more to drink, shaking his head. Kiko smoked some bizarre shit, and I always had to spray honey-suckle deodorizer the next day to make the smell go away.

Months went by. Myriam came over more and more of-ten, and almost always alone. She and Fanny would shut themselves in the bedroom, and I'd hear them chuckling until the wee hours. One night when I went in to ask if they wanted some herbal tea or anything, I found them both stretched out on the floor listening to an old Jean-Jacques Goldman cassette: "Siiiince you're leaeaeavv-iiing . . . and nyanyanya."

Pathetic.

Sometimes Myriam went away again. Sometimes not.

There was an extra toothbrush in the Duralex glass in the bathroom, and the sofa bed was often unfolded at night.

And then one day, she said:

"If it's Kiko, say I'm not here . . ." pointing to the phone.

And then, and then, and then . . . One morning, she asked me:

"Would you mind if I crash with you guys for a while? . . . I'll chip in toward expenses, of course. . . ."

I was being careful not to break my biscotti—because if there's one thing I hate, it's to break my biscottis. I told her:

"No problem."

"Cool. Thanks."

"Just one thing . . ."

"What's that?"

"Do you think you could go out on the balcony when you smoke? . . . "

She smiled, got up, and gave me a big artist's smack.

Of course, my biscotti broke and I said to myself, "And so it begins . . . ," stirring my hot cocoa to retrieve the little pieces. But even so, I was happy.

Still, it bothered me all day, and so that night I laid it all out. "We'll share the rent, as much as possible, and we'll divvy up the shopping, cooking, and cleaning. Okay, girls? Look at the refrigerator door, I've posted a calendar with our weeks: Fanny, you're in pink highlighter, Myriam, you're in blue, and I'm in yellow. . . . Please let the rest of us know if you're eating out or if you're having guests, and speaking of guests, if you bring home guys you plan to sleep with, please work it out between the two of you for who gets the bedroom when. And . . ."

"All right, enough . . . enough. . . . Don't get ex-
cited . . . ," said Myriam.

"No kidding . . . ," her sister answered.

"And what about you? When you bring home some
little chick, be nice and give us fair warning, too, okay!
So we can get rid of our fishnet stockings and our old
condoms. . . ."

And they snickered even harder.

Damn.

Our little arrangement worked out pretty well, for the
most part. I'll admit I didn't really think it would, but I
was wrong. . . . When girls want something to work out,
it works out. It's just that simple.

When I look back on it now, I realize just how much it
meant to Fanny to have Myriam here.

Fanny's the total opposite of her sister. She's romantic
and faithful—and sensitive.

She's always falling in love with some inaccessible guy
who lives in Bumblefuck. Ever since she was fifteen, she's
waited impatiently for the mail every morning and done
flips every time the phone rang.

That's no way to live.

First there was Fabrice, who lived in Lille. (From Tulle, you can see the difficulty. . . .) He drowned her under a flood of passionate letters in which he only talked about himself. Four years of frustrated, juvenile love.

Next, there was Paul, who went off to somewhere in Burkina Faso with Doctors Without Borders, leaving her with the beginnings of a vocation, the energy to rail against the slowness of the post office, and all her tears to cry. . . . Five years of frustrated, exotic love.

And now the last straw: I thought I gathered from their late-night conversations and the allusions they made at the dinner table that Fanny was in love with a doctor who was already married.

I could hear them in the bathroom. Myriam, brushing her teeth, said to her:

"He'sch got kidsch?"

I imagine that Fanny was sitting on the toilet seat cover. "No."

"That'sch bescht becausche . . ." (she spits) ". . . with kids that'd be too much of a pain in the ass, you know. Anyway, I could never do it."

Fanny didn't answer, but I'm sure that she was chewing on her hair and looking at the bath mat or her toes.

"It's like you go looking for them. . . ."

". . ."

"We've had it up to here with your fucking star-crossed lovers. Plus, doctors are all bores. Later he'll take up golf, and then he'll always be stuck in meetings at the Morocco Club Med or wherever, and you'll still be all alone. . . ."

". . ."

"Plus, lemme tell you. . . . Maybe it'll work out—it's possible—but what makes you think it will? . . . Because the Other Woman, do you really think she's going to let go of her guy just like that? 'Cause she likes tanning in Morocco, so she can one-up the dentist's wife from the Rotary Club."

Fanny must be smiling—you can hear it in her voice. She murmurs:

"I'm sure you're right. . . ."

"Of course I'm right!"

Six months of frustrated, adulterous love. (Maybe.)

"So come with me to the Galerie Delaunay on Saturday night. For one thing, I know the guy who's doing the catering, and it won't be bad. I'm sure Marc will be there. . . . I absolutely have to introduce you two! You'll see—he's a great guy! Plus he's got a fabulous ass."

"Pschsch, whatever. . . . What kind of show is it?"

"I don't remember. Hey, couldja hand me the towel?"

Myriam often improved upon the ordinary by bringing home little dishes from Fauchon's and fine wines. I have to admit, she'd hit again on an outrageous scheme. For several weeks, she'd pored over books and magazines on Lady Di—you couldn't cross the living room without stepping on the deceased—and practiced drawing her. Now, every weekend, she planted her gear on the pont de l'Alma and sketched the weepy-eyed from around the world next to their idol.

For a ludicrous amount of money ("stupidity has its price"), a Japanese tourist on one of those big group tours could ask my sister to draw her next to a laughing Diana (at a party at Harry's school) or a crying Diana (with Belfast AIDS patients) or a Diana showing sympathy (with the Liverpool AIDS patients) or a Diana sulking (at the commemoration of the fifty-year anniversary of the Landing).

I salute the artist and take charge of bringing the bottles to room temperature.

Yes, our arrangement was working out well. Fanny and I didn't talk much more than before, but we laughed more. Myriam didn't settle down any at all, but she painted. To my sisters, I seemed like the perfect guy—although not the one they'd have wanted to marry.

I didn't give it much thought. I just shrugged my shoulders and kept an eye on the oven door.

So it took a fistful of lingerie to bowl a strike.

It would mean the end of the evenings seated at the foot of the couch, watching my sisters and sighing. The end of Fanny's made-on-call cocktails, which unsettle your stomach and remind you of all kinds of salacious stories. The end of the squabbles:

"Well, *think* of it! Shit! It's important—was his name Lilian or Tristan?"

"I don't know. He doesn't articulate very well, this guy of yours. . . ."

"You're impossible! Are you doing this on purpose, or what? Try to remember!"

" 'Hello, may I speak to Myriam? It's Ltfrgzqan.' That better?"

And she disappeared into the kitchen.

"Please don't slam the refrigerator door. . . ."
Bang.

". . . Maybe you could give him the name of a good speech therapist. . . ."

"Chmmchmpoordjit."

"Hey, you know, it wouldn't do you any harm, either."
Bang.

The end of making up over my famous chicken Boursin.
("Well? . . . Don't you think you're better off here with us
than off with Ltfrgzqan at some cheesy idiot fest?")

The end of the highlighted calendar weeks, the end of
Saturday-morning shopping trips, the end of the *Gala*
magazines sitting in the bathroom open to the horo-
scope pages, the end of the artists of all kinds trying to get
us to understand Boltanski's rags, the end of the all-
nighters, the end of helping Fanny memorize her study
sheets, the end of the stress the days the results were
posted, the end of the black looks for the woman who
lived downstairs, the end of the Jeff Buckley songs, the
end of Sundays stretched out on the carpet reading the
comics, the end of the Haribo candy orgies in front of
the TV, watching *Sacrée Soirée*, the end of the toothpaste
tubes with the caps never on, drying out and driving me
crazy.

The end of my youth.

We'd planned a dinner to celebrate the end of
Fanny's exams. She was beginning to see the light at the
end of the tunnel. . . .

"Whew! Only ten more years . . . ," she said, smiling.

Around the coffee table were her internist (without his wedding ring, the coward—future golfer in Morocco, I still say) and her girlfriends from the hospital, including the famous Laura. My sisters had cooked up an incalculable number of plans for the two of us, each more inane than the next, under the pretext that she'd spoken about me one day with a tremor in her voice. (Like the time they had me go to her house for a surprise birthday party and I found myself alone all evening with this fury, hunting for contacts in the goat-hair carpet while trying to protect my ass. . . .)

Marc was there, too. (I took advantage to see what "a fabulous ass" is . . . so–so. . . .)

There were also some friends of Myriam's that I'd never seen before.

I wondered where she dug up such freaks—guys tattooed from head to toe and girls mounted on stilts you wouldn't believe, laughing at everything and shaking whatever it was they had instead of hair.

My sisters had said:

"Bring your friends from work if you want. . . . You know, you never introduce us to anyone. . . ."

And for good reason, I thought later, admiring the flora

and the fauna eating my peanuts, sprawled out on the Cinna couch that Mom gave me when I got my accounting degree. *And for good reason. . . .*

It was already pretty late, and we were all good and wasted, when Myriam—who'd gone to look for a scented candle in my room—came back gobbling like a turkey in heat, with Sarah Briot's bra between her thumb and forefinger.

Holy shit.

Now I was in for it.

"Hey, but what's this?! Wait, Olivier, 'dja know you've got sex-shop props in your room? . . . Something to make every guy in Paris pitch a tent! Don't tell us you didn't know!?"

And off she goes putting on a whole damn show, out of control.

She wiggles her hips, mimes a striptease, sniffs the panties, grips the halogen lamp, and falls over backward.

Out of control.

Everyone else is dying of laughter. Even the golf champ.

"Okay. That's enough," I said. "Give me that."

"Who's it for? First you have to tell us who it's for . . . doesn't he, guys?"

So all those jackasses start whistling with their fingers,

clicking their teeth against their glasses, and worst of all messing up my living room!

"Plus, did you see the hooters she's got! Look, that's gotta be at least a thirty-six!" yells this moron Laura.

"You won't get bored, huh . . . ," Fanny whispered, her mouth twisting bizarrely.

I got up. I took my keys and jacket and slammed the door.

Bang.

I slept at the Ibis hotel at La Porte de Versailles.

No, I didn't sleep. I thought.

I spent a good part of the night standing at the window, my forehead pressed against the glass, looking at the Parc des Expositions.

How ugly.

By morning, my mind was made up. I wasn't even hung-over, and I put away a huge breakfast.

I went to the flea market.

I hardly ever take time for myself.

I was like a tourist in Paris. I had my hands in my

pockets and I smelled good: Nina Ricci's aftershave for men, found in all the Ibis hotels around the world. I'd have loved to run into my colleague at a bend in the path:

"Oh, Olivier!"

"Oh, Sarah!"

"Oh, Olivier, you smell so good. . . ."

"Oh, Sarah!"

I sat on the terrace at the Café des Amis, a beer in front of me, drinking in the sun.

It was June 16, about noon. It was a gorgeous day and my life was beautiful.

I bought an overornate birdcage with lots of iron flourishes.

The guy who sold it to me assured me that it dated from the nineteenth century and that it had belonged to a very highly esteemed family, since it had been found in a private mansion, still in one piece, and so on and so forth and how are you paying?

I felt like saying, *Don't wear yourself out, old man, I couldn't care less.*

When I got back home, it smelled like Mr. Clean from the ground floor up.

The apartment was spotless. Not a speck of dust. There was even a bouquet on the kitchen table with a little note: "We're at the Jardin des Plantes—see you tonight. XOXO."

I took off my watch and set it down on my bedside table. The Christian Dior package was right there next to it, as if nothing had happened.

Aaahhh!! My dears. . . .

For dinner, I'm going to make a chicken Boursin that will be un-for-get-ta-ble.

Okay, first I've got to choose the wine . . . and put out a tablecloth, of course.

And for dessert, a semolina cake with lots of rum. Fanny loves that.

I'm not saying we threw our arms around each other, squeezing each other tight and shaking our heads, the way Americans do. They just gave me a little smile as they came in, and I saw all the little flowers of the Jardin des Plantes in their faces.

For once, we weren't in any rush to clear the table. After the debauchery of the night before, no one had any plans to go out, and Mimi served us mint tea at the kitchen table.

"What's with the cage?" asked Fanny.

"I bought it at the flea market this morning from this guy who doesn't sell anything but antique cages. . . . Do you like it?"

"Yes."

"Good, it's for the two of you."

"Really! Thank you. What's the occasion—because we're so full of tact and sensitivity?" joked Myriam, heading for the balcony with her pack of Cravens.

"As a souvenir of me. You have only to say that the bird has flown his cage. . . ."

"Why are you saying that?!"

"I'm leaving, girls."

"Where are you going?"

"I'm going to go live somewhere else."

"With who?"

"On my own."

"But why? It's because of last night. . . . Listen, I am so sorry—you know I had too much to drink, and . . ."

"No, no, don't worry about it. It's got nothing to do with you."

Fanny seemed really stunned, and I had a hard time looking her in the face.

"You're tired of us?"

"No, that's not it."

"But why, then?" You could tell the tears were coming to her eyes.

Myriam stood rooted between the table and the window, her cigarette hanging sadly from her lips.

"Olivier, hey—what's going on?"

"I'm in love."

You couldn't just say so right away, you jerk.

And why haven't you introduced us? What! You're afraid we'll scare her off. You don't know us very well. . . . Oh? You do know us well. . . . Ah?

What's her name?

Is she pretty? Yes? Oh, shit. . . .

What? You've barely even spoken to her? Are you an idiot, or what? Yes, you are an idiot?

No, you're not.

You've barely even spoken to her, and you're moving out because of her? Don't you think you're putting the cart before the horse? You put the cart where you can. . . . Well, if you look at it that way, of course. . . .

When are you going to talk to her? Someday. Okay, I see the problem. . . . Does she have a good sense of humor? Ah, good, good.

You really love her? You don't want to answer that?

Are we annoying you?

All you have to do is say so.

You'll invite us to the wedding? Only if we promise to be good?

Who's going to make me feel better the next time my heart turns to mush?

And me? Who's going to make me study for my anatomy class?

Who's going to pamper us now?

Just how pretty is she?

Are you going to make her your chicken au Boursin?

We're going to miss you, you know.

I was surprised that I had so few things to take with me. I'd rented a small van from Kiloutou's, and one trip was enough.

I didn't know if I should take that in a good way, as in, *Well, that just proves you're not too attached to the things of this world, my friend,* or really badly, as in, *Look, friend: you're almost thirty, and eleven boxes for everything you've got. . . . Doesn't amount to much, does it?*

Before I left, I sat down one last time in the kitchen.

The first couple of weeks, I slept on a mattress right on the floor. I'd read in a magazine that it's very good for your back.

After seventeen days, I went to Ikea. My back was hurting too much.

God knows I'd considered the problem from every possible angle. I even drew out floor plans on graph paper.

The saleswoman thought the same thing I did: In an apartment so modest and so poorly laid out (you'd have thought I'd rented three little hallways . . .), a sofa bed was the way to go.

And the least expensive kind is the Clic-Clac.

A Clic-Clac it is.

I also bought a kitchen set (sixty-five pieces for sixty euros, salad spinner and cheese grater included), some candles (you never know . . .), a plaid throw (I don't know, I thought it would be chic to buy a plaid throw), a lamp (whatever), a doormat (thinking ahead), some shelves (predictably), a green plant (we'll see . . .), and a thousand other little things. (That's how the store wants it.)

Myriam and Fanny leave regular messages on my answering machine: *Beeeep* "How do you turn on the oven?" *beeeeep* "We got the oven on but now we're wondering how to change a fuse because everything blew. . . ." *beeeeep* "We're ready to do what you said but where do you keep the flashlight? . . ." *beeeep* "Hey, what's the number for the fire department?" *beeep* . . .

I think they're exaggerating a little, but—like all people who live alone—I've learned to check and even hope for the little red blinking message light when I come home in the evenings.

I don't think anyone escapes that.

And then suddenly, your life speeds up like crazy.

And when I lose control of a situation, I tend to panic. It's stupid.

So, what do I mean by "losing control of the situation"?

Losing control of the situation is very simple. It's having Sarah Briot show up one morning in the room where you make your living by the sweat of your brow and seat herself on the edge of your desk, hitching up her skirt.

And saying:

"Your glasses are dirty, aren't they?"

And pulling a little hem of pink shirt out from under her skirt and wiping your glasses with it, like it's nothing.

Then you pop such a glorious boner you could lift the desk with it (with a little training of course).

"So, I hear you've moved?"

"Yeah, a couple of weeks ago."

(Ffffff . . . breathe . . . Everything's going fine. . . .)

"Where are you now?"

"In the tenth arrondissement."

"Oh! That's funny—me, too."

"Really?!"

"That's good—now we'll be riding the same metro. . . ."

(It's a start.)

"Aren't you going to have a housewarming party or something?"

"Yes—yes, of course!"

(News to me.)

"When?"

"Oh, well, I don't know yet. . . . You know, I just had the last of my furniture delivered this morning, so . . ."

"What about tonight?"

"Tonight? Oh, no, tonight won't work. The place is a mess, and . . . and then, that doesn't give people much notice, and . . ."

"You don't have to invite anyone but me. Because, you know, I don't care about the mess—it can't be any worse than my place! . . ."

"Oh . . . well . . . well, if you want. But not too early, then?!"

"Great—that way I'll have time to stop by my place to change. . . . How about nine o'clock—does that work for you?"

"Nine o'clock, great."

"Okay, well, see you later, then? . . ."

That's what I mean by "losing control of the situation."

I left early, and for the first time in my life, I didn't straighten up my desk before I put out the light.

The concierge was watching for me: "Yes, they delivered your furniture, but what an ordeal to get that couch up six flights!"

"Thanks, Madame Rodriguez, thanks." (I won't forget your Christmas bonus, Madame Rodriguez. . . .)

Three little corridors shaped like a battlefield. . . . It's got its charms. . . .

Put the taramasalata in a cool place, heat up the coq au vin, over low heat, okay . . . open the bottles, set a makeshift table, race back down to the convenience store to get paper napkins and a bottle of mineral water, set up the coffeemaker, take a shower, put on cologne (Eau Sauvage), clean your ears, find a shirt that's not too wrinkled, turn down the lamp, unplug the phone, put on some music (Rickie Lee Jones's *Pirates* album—anything's possible with that . . . but not too loud), arrange the plaid throw, light the candles (well, well . . .), breathe in, breathe out, don't look at yourself anymore in the mirror.

And the condoms? (In the drawer of the bedside table—isn't that too close? . . . And in the bathroom, isn't that too far? . . .)

Dring, dring.

Is it fair to say I've got the situation in hand?

Sarah Briot came in. Pretty as the day.

Later in the evening, when we'd had a few good laughs, eaten well, and let some dreamy silences set in, it was clear that Sarah Briot would be spending the night in my arms.

Only I've always had trouble making certain decisions— and yet, it was *really* time to put down my glass and make a move.

Like if Roger Rabbit's wife were sitting right next to you, and you were thinking about your savings plan. . . .

She was talking about I don't know what and looking at me out of the corner of her eye.

And suddenly . . . suddenly . . . I thought about this couch that we were sitting on.

I began to really, intensely, steadily wonder: How do you open up a Clic-Clac?

I thought it would be best to begin by kissing her fairly passionately and then to tilt her back deftly in order to lay her down without incident. . . .

Yes, but afterward . . . with the Clic-Clac?

I could already see myself getting silently worked up over some little latch while her tongue tickled my tonsils and her hands searched for my belt. . . .

Well . . . for the moment, that wasn't exactly the case. . . . She was even beginning to stifle the beginnings of a yawn. . . .

Some Don Juan. What a disgrace.

And then I thought of my sisters. I laughed inside thinking of those two harpies.

They'd have had a ball if they could've seen me just then, with Miss Universe's thigh up against mine and me getting all worked up about how to open the sofa bed from Ikea.

Just then, Sarah Briot turned to me and said:

"You're cute when you smile."

And she kissed me.

And then, at that exact moment, with 119 pounds of femininity on my knees, all sweetness and caresses, I closed my eyes, threw my head back, and thought with all my might: "Thank you, girls."

Epilogue

"Marguerite! When are we eating?"
"Screw you."

Since I've been writing stories, my husband's started calling me Marguerite—for Marguerite Duras—as he taps
me on the ass. He tells everyone at dinner parties that he's
going to stop working soon, thanks to my royalties:

"Listen . . . as far as I'm concerned, no problem! I'm
just waiting for it all to pan out, and I'll go pick up the
kids from school in my Jaguar XK8. It's all set. . . . Of
course, I'll have to massage her shoulders from time to
time and put up with her little crises of doubt, but
hey . . . that coupe? . . . I'll take it in dragon green."

He keeps raving about it, and people don't know how
to take it.

They say to me, in the tone you'd use to talk about a sexually transmitted disease:

"Is that true—you write?"

And I just shrug my shoulders, showing my glass to the master of the house. I grumble out a *No, whatever, almost nothing.* And Mr. Excitable, whom I married in a moment of weakness, just keeps laying it on:

"Wait. . . . Didn't she tell you? Sweetie, didn't you tell them about the prize you won at Saint-Quentin? Hey! . . . Fifteen hundred euros, you know!!! Two nights at her computer, which she bought for seventy-five euros at a charity sale, and fifteen hundred euros fall into our laps! . . . What more could you ask? And I'm not even telling you about all her other prizes . . . huh, Pumpkin, let's stay humble."

It's true that at these moments, I really want to kill him.

But I won't.

First of all because he weighs a hundred and eighty pounds (he says one seventy-five—pure coquetry), and then also because he's right.

He's right—and what will become of me if I start believing in it too much?

I quit my job? I finally say some nasty things to my coworker Micheline? I buy myself a little zobi-skin notebook and I take notes *for later*? I feel so alone, so far away, so close, so *different*? I go meditate at the tomb of Chateaubriand? I say: "No, not tonight, please, my head's bursting"? I forget to show up at day care because I have a chapter to finish?

You should see the kids at the day-care center from five-thirty on. You ring the bell, and they all rush to the door, hearts pounding. The one who opens it is inevitably disappointed to see you, since you're not there for him, but after the first second of despair (mouth twisted, shoulders drooping, and blankie trailing on the ground again), he turns to your son (just behind him) and yells:

"Louis, it's your mom!!!!!"

And so then you hear:

"Well, yeah . . . I doh."

But Marguerite is getting tired of all these pretenses.

She wants to be clear in her own mind about it. If she's going to have to go to Combourg to track down Chateaubriand's grave, she might as well find out right away.

She chose some stories (two sleepless nights), she printed them out with her antiquated machine (more than three hours to do a hundred and thirty-four pages!), she clutched her sheets of paper to her heart and took them to the copy shop over by the law school. She stood in line behind noisy coeds perched on high heels (she felt old and frumpy, our Marguerite).

The salesgirl asked:

"A white binder or a black binder?"

And there she was, fretting all over again. (White? That's a little too much like a goody-goody communicant, isn't it? . . . But black, that's way too self-assured, more like a doctoral thesis, isn't it? . . . Misery of miseries.)

Finally the young woman loses patience:

"What is it exactly?"

"Some stories . . ."

"News stories? About what?"

"No, not news stories . . . short stories, you know? . . . It's to send to a publisher. . . ."

". . . ??? . . . Yeah . . . well, okay, that doesn't really tell us what color binding . . ."

"Use whichever one you want—I'll leave it to you." (*Alea jacta est.*)

"Well, in that case, I'll give you the turquoise, because right now it's on sale: four euros fifty cents instead of five twenty-five . . . (A turquoise binder on the chic desk of an elegant Left Bank publisher . . . whoops.)

"Okay, go with the turquoise." (Don't stand in the way of Destiny, my girl.)

The girl lifts up the cover of her big Xerox machine and manhandles the packet like so many vulgar handouts on civil law: there you go, I'll just turn it every which way for you, and there you go, I'll just dog-ear the corners for you.

The artist suffers in silence.

As the girl takes the money, she picks up the cigarette she'd left on the cash register and asks:

"What are they about, your stories?"

"Everything."

"Oh."

". . ."

". . ."

"But mostly about love."

"Oh?"

She buys a magnificent envelope made out of kraft paper. The sturdiest, most beautiful, most expensive one, with padded corners and an unassailable flap. The Rolls of envelopes.

She goes to the post office and asks for collectors' stamps—the prettiest ones, the ones that show works of modern art. She licks them lovingly, gracefully presses them on, casts a spell on the envelope, blesses it, makes the sign of the cross over it, and utters some other incantations that must remain secret.

She goes up to the letter slot marked "Paris and suburbs only." She kisses her treasure one last time, turns away her eyes, and abandons it.

Across from the post office, there's a bar. She leans her elbows on the counter, orders a calvados. She doesn't really like them, but hey, she has her status as an accursed artist to uphold now. She lights a cigarette, and from this moment on, you could say, she waits.

I didn't say anything to anyone.

"Hey—what are you doing with the key to the mailbox on a chain around your neck?"

"Nothing."

"Hey—what are you doing holding all those Castorama fliers?"

"Nothing."

"Hey—what are you doing with the mailman's satchel?"

"Nothing, I'm telling you! . . ."

"Wait . . . are you in love with him or what?!"

No. I didn't say anything. Can you see me answering: "I'm waiting for an answer from a publisher." The shame.

Anyway . . . it's crazy the junk mail you get these days—it's really just whatever.

And then there's work, and then there's Micheline and her fake nails attached poorly, and then there's the geraniums to bring in, and then the Walt Disney tapes, the little electric train, and the season's first visit to the pediatrician, and then the dog shedding, and Robert McLiam Wilson's *Eureka Street* to measure the immeasurable, and then movies, and family and friends, and then still other emotions (but nothing much next to *Eureka Street*, it's true).

Our Marguerite resigned herself to hibernation.

Three months later.
Hallelujah!
Hallelujah! Hallelu-u-u-jah!

It came.
The letter.
It's a bit light.
I slide it under my sweater and call my Kiki:
"Kiiiiiiiikiiiiiiii!!!"
I go to read it all alone, in the silence and meditation of the little wooded area next door, which serves as a

pooping ground for all the dogs in the neighborhood. (Note that even in moments like this, I remain lucid.)

"*Madame* blablabla, *it is with great interest that* blablabla *and that's why* blablabla *I would like to meet with you* blablabla, *please get in touch with my secretary* blablabla *I'm looking forward to* blablabla *dear madame* blablabla. . . ."

I savor it.

I savor it.

I savor it.

The vengeance of Marguerite has struck.

"Honey?" I ask my husband, "When are we eating?"

"??? . . . What are you asking me for? What's going on?"

"Oh, nothing—it's just that I won't have much time for cooking anymore, what with all the fan letters I'll have to answer, not to mention the festivals, the conventions, the book fairs . . . all those trips all over France and in the overseas territories, oh la la. . . . God. Come to think of it, I'll have to start getting regular manicures soon, because, you know . . . for the book signings, it's important to have impeccable hands. . . . It's crazy how people get hung up on that. . . ."

"What are you raving about?"

Marguerite lets the letter from the elegant Left Bank publisher "escape" onto the potbellied stomach of her husband, who's reading the classifieds in *Auto Plus*.

"Hold on . . . hey! What is this?!"

"Nothing—I haven't had it for long. It's just something I have to tell Micheline. Go make yourself handsome: I'm taking you to the Aigle Noir tonight. . . ."

"The Aigle Noir!?"

"Yes. That's where Marguerite would have taken her Yann, I suppose. . . ."

"Who's Yann?"

"Pfffff, forget it. . . . You don't know the first *thing* about the literary world."

So I got in contact with the secretary. A very good contact, I think, because the young woman was more than charming.

Maybe she had a fluorescent pink Post-it stuck in front of her eyes: "If A.G. calls, be *very* charming!" underlined twice.

Maybe . . .

The poor dears, they must think I sent my stories to others. . . . They're afraid someone's going to beat them to it. Another publisher, even more elegant, situated on an even more chic street on the Left Bank, with a secretary who's even more charming on the phone and who has an even cuter ass.

Oh, no, that would be too unfair.

You see the disaster if I hit the big time under another imprint just because what's-her-name didn't have a fluorescent pink Post-it in front of her eyes?

I don't dare think about it.

The appointment was set for one week later. (We've all wasted enough time.)

The initial pragmatic concerns were soon out of the way: taking an afternoon off ("Micheline, I won't be in tomorrow!"); making arrangements for the kids—but not just anywhere, in a place where they'll be happy; informing my love:

"I'm going into Paris tomorrow."

"Why?"

"On business."

"Is it a romantic tryst?"

"Same difference."

"Who is it?"

"The mailman."

"Ah! I should have known. . . ."

. . . Leaving the one truly important problem: what am I going to wear?

Something that says true future writer, devoid of elegance because the *real* life is somewhere else. Don't love me for my big breasts; love me for my substantive marrow.

Something that says true future best-seller-writing machine, with a perm, because the real life is right here. Don't love me for my talent; love me for my tabloid potential.

Something that says woman-who-eats-up-elegant-men-from-the-Left-Bank, get it while it's hot, because the real life is on your desk. Don't love me for my manuscript; love me for my stunning marrow.

Hey, Atala, calm down.

In the end, the stress is too much for me—you know, this really isn't the time to be thinking about playing footsie and losing a stocking on the rug. This is undoubtedly the most momentous day of my tiny existence, and I'm not going to jeopardize the whole thing with some outfit that's undeniably irresistible but totally cumbersome.

(Well, yeah! A mini miniskirt is cumbersome.)

I'll wear jeans. Nothing more, nothing less. My trusty 501s, ten years old, barrel-aged, stonewashed, with copper rivets and the reddish label on the right butt-cheek. The pair that have taken my shape and my scent. My friend.

Even so, I get nervous when I think about this elegant, brilliant man who juggles my future in his slender hands. (Publish her? Don't publish her?) . . . Jeans are pushing it a little, I have to admit.

Oh . . . nothing but worries, nothing but worries.

Okay, I've made up my mind. Jeans, but with lingerie to knock your socks off.

But he won't even see that, you tell me. . . . Don't tut-tut-tut me—you don't get to the Very High Post of Publisher without having a special gift for detecting the most improbable, fine lingerie.

No, these men know.

They know if the woman seated across from them is wearing some cotton thing that comes up to her belly button, or cheap pink panties from Monoprix, all stretched out of shape, or one of those extravagant little things that make women redden (the price they pay for them) and men turn pink (the price they're going to have to pay).

Of course they know.

And this time, let me tell you, I spared no expense (payable in two installments). I got a coordinating bra-and-panty set—something out of this world.

God . . .

Super nice stuff, super material, super cut—all in ivory silk with Calais lace, hand-knitted by little old French ladies, if you please. Soft, pretty, refined, tender, unforgettable. The sort of thing that melts in your mouth and not in your hand.

Destiny, here I am.

Looking at myself in the mirror at the shop (the fiends, they've got special lighting that makes you look thin and tan—the same halogens they use over the dead fish in the gourmet supermarkets), I told myself for the first time since Marguerite has existed:

"Well, then, I don't regret all that time I spent biting my nails, and getting eczema in front of my tiny computer screen. Oh, no! All that, all those times I wore myself out arm-wrestling against the fear and the lack of self-confidence, all those scraps in my head and all those things I lost or forgot because I was thinking about 'Clic-Clac,' for example—well, I don't regret them. . . ."

I can't tell you exactly how much I spent, what with being politically correct—my husband's dental bridge, car insurance, the rising tax for welfare, and all that—I'd risk shocking you. But know that it's something staggering; and, given what it weighs, let's not talk about the price per pound.

After all, nothing comes from nothing, you can't catch flies with vinegar, and you can't get yourself published without giving a little of yourself, don't you think?

Here we are: the sixth arrondissement of Paris.

The district where you find as many writers as meter maids. At the heart of life.

I'm losing my nerve.

My stomach hurts, my chest hurts, my legs hurt, I'm sweating buckets, and my ***-euro panties are riding up.

Pretty picture.

I get lost, the street name isn't posted anywhere, there are galleries of African art in every direction, and nothing looks more like an African mask than another African mask. I'm beginning to hate African art.

Finally, I find my way.

They make me wait.

I think I'm going to pass out. I breathe like they taught us for having a baby. Okay . . . now . . . calm . . . down. . . .

Sit up straight. Watch. You can always learn something. Breathe in. Breathe out.

"Are you feeling all right?"

"Uh . . . yes, yes . . . I'm fine."

"*He*'s in a meeting, but *He* won't be much longer. *He*'ll be here in just a little while. . . ."

". . ."

"Would you like a cup of coffee?"

"No. Thank you." (Hey, what's-your-name, can't you see I want to throw up? Help me—a slap, a bucket, a bowl, a Pepto-Bismol, a glass of nice cold soda . . . something. I'm begging you.)

A smile. She gives me a smile.

In fact, it was curiosity. Neither more nor less.

He wanted to see me. He wanted to see what I looked like. He wanted to see what sort of person would write this stuff.

That's all.

I'm not going to tell you about the interview. At the moment, I'm treating my eczema with nearly pure tar, and it's really not worth aggravating it, given the color of my bathtub. So I won't tell you about it.

Well, okay . . . maybe just a little bit: After a while, the cat (for further details, see "Lucifer" in *Cinderella*), who was watching the mouse gesticulating every which way between his clawed paws . . . the cat, who was having fun ("isn't she unsophisticated, after all") . . . the cat, who was taking his time, finished by saying:

"Listen, I'll be honest with you: Your manuscript does some interesting things, and you do have a *certain* style, but" (next come more than a few reflections on people who write in general and the hard job of a publisher in particular) ". . . The way things are now, and for reasons I'm sure you'll understand, we can't publish your manuscript. On the other hand, I'd like to follow your work very closely—and I want you to know that I'll always give it my utmost attention. There."

There.

Jackass.

I stay seated, stunned. There's no other word for it.

He gets up (with sweeping, magnificent gestures), heads toward me, and makes as if to shake my hand. . . . Not seeing any reaction on my part, he makes as if to offer me his hand. . . . Not seeing any reaction on my part, he makes as if to take my hand. . . . Not seeing any . . .

"What's going on? Come on . . . don't be so depressed—you know, it's extremely rare to get a first manuscript published. You know, I have confidence in you. I can tell we're going to do great things together. In fact, I'll be honest with you: I'm *counting* on you."

Stop the chariots, Ben-Hur. Can't you tell I'm stuck?

"Listen, I'm sorry. I don't know what's happened, but I can't get up. It's like all my strength's gone. It's stupid."

"Does this happen often?"

"No. It's the first time."

"Does it hurt?"

"No. Well, a little, but that's something else."

"Wiggle your fingers, just to see."

"I can't."

"You're sure?"

"Well . . . yes."

A long exchange of looks, like a couple of kids having a staring contest.

(irritated) "Are you doing this on purpose or what?"

(very irritated) "Well, of course not, for heaven's sake!!"

"Do you want me to call a doctor?"

"No, no, it'll pass."

"Yes, well, okay, then. . . . The problem is, I've got other meetings. . . . You can't stay here."

". . ."

"Try again. . . ."

"Nothing."

"What is this business?"

"I don't know. . . . What do you want me to say? . . . Maybe it's an arthritis attack or something, triggered by overwhelming emotions."

"If I tell you, 'Okay, fine, I'll publish you' . . . will you get up?"

"Of course not. What do you take me for? Do I really seem that moronic?"

"No, but I mean if I really do publish you? . . ."

"First of all, I wouldn't believe you. . . . Hey, wait, I'm not here to beg your charity—I'm paralyzed. Can't you understand the difference?"

(rubbing his face in his slender hands) "And it had to happen to me. . . . Good God . . ."

". . ."

(looking at his watch) "Listen, for the moment, I'm going to move you, because I really need my office now. . . ."

So then he pushes me down the hall as if I were in a wheelchair, except that I'm not in a wheelchair—and for him, that must make a hell of a difference. . . . I settle in good.

Suffer, my friend. Suffer.

"Would you like a cup of coffee now?"

"Yes, I'd love one. That's nice of you."

"Are you sure you don't want me to call a doctor?"

"No, no. Thank you. It'll go away just the way it came on."

"You're too tense."

"I know."

What's-her-name never had a pink Post-it stuck on her phone. She was charming to me the other day because she's a girl who *is* charming.

Today won't have been a total waste.

It's true. You don't often get the chance to watch a girl like her for hours on end.

I love her voice.

From time to time, she makes little signs to me so I'll feel less alone.

And then the computers were shut down, the answering machines were set up, the lights were turned off, and the office was emptied.

I saw them all leave, one after another, and they all thought I was there because I had an appointment. Whatever.

Finally Blue-Beard came out of the lair where he makes the little writer wannabees cry.

"You're still here!!"

". . ."

"What am I going to do with you?"

"I don't know."

"Well, I do. I'm going to call the ambulance or the fire department and they're going to get you out of here in the next five minutes! You don't plan on sleeping here, do you?!"

"No, don't call anyone, please. . . . It's going to come unstuck, I can feel it. . . ."

"Sure, but I've got to lock up—you can understand that, can't you?"

"Then take me down to the sidewalk."

You might have guessed, he's not the one who took me down. He hailed a couple of messenger boys nearby. Two tall, handsome guys—tattooed footmen for my sedan chair.

They each took an armrest and deposited me gently at the foot of the building.

Too cute.

My ex–future publisher, this tactful man who's *counting* on me in the future, said his good-byes with lots of panache.

He walked away, turning back several times and shaking his head like he was trying to wake up from a bad dream—no, truly, he really couldn't believe it.

At least he'll have something to talk about at dinner.

It's his wife who'll be happy. For once he won't talk her ear off about the crisis in publishing.

For the first time all day, I felt good.

I watched the waiters at the restaurant across the street fussing around their damask tablecloths. They were very stylish (like my stories, I thought, snickering)—especially one, whom I watched closely.

Exactly the sort of French *garçon de café* who upsets the hormonal systems of fat American women in Reeboks.

I smoked an exceptionally good cigarette, expelling the smoke slowly and watching the passersby.

I was almost happy—aside from a few details, like the presence of a parking meter on my right that smelled like dog piss.

How long did I stay there, contemplating my disaster?

I don't know.

The restaurant was at its peak, and you could see couples seated on the terrace, laughing as they drank glasses of rosé.

I couldn't stop myself from thinking:

. . . In another life, maybe, my publisher would've taken me to lunch there "because it's so practical." He'd have made me laugh, too, and suggested a much better wine than that Côteaux de Provence. . . . He'd have pressed me to finish my novel, "surprisingly mature for a young woman your age . . . ," and then he'd have taken my arm and escorted me to a taxi stand. He would have romanced me a little. . . .

. . . In another life. Surely.

Well, okay. . . . It's not everything, Marguerite. I've got ironing waiting for me. . . .

I got up with a bound, pulling at my jeans, and headed toward a gorgeous young woman sitting on the base of a statue of Auguste Comte.

Look at her.

Beautiful, sensual, full-blooded, with flawless legs and very fine ankles, her nose turned up, her forehead rounded, her allure fierce and warlike.

Wearing some string and tattoos.

Lips and nails painted black.

An incredible girl.

She threw regular, irritated looks in the direction of the adjacent street. I think her lover must've been late.

I handed her my manuscript.

"Take it," I said, "it's a gift. To help pass the time."

I think she thanked me, but I'm not sure—because she wasn't French! . . . Distressed by this little detail, I nearly took back my magnificent gift, and then . . . What for? I said to myself. And as I walked away, I was even rather content.

From here on out, my manuscript was in the hands of the most beautiful girl in the world.

That consoled me.

A little.